Mouse Woman
and the
Mischief-Makers

Mouse Woman
and the
Mischief-Makers

by

CHRISTIE HARRIS

DRAWINGS BY DOUGLAS TAIT

Atheneum · New York

1977

Library of Congress Cataloging in Publication Data

Harris, Christie.
Mouse woman and the mischief-makers.

Summary: More stories of how Mouse Woman, the tiny
character, part mouse, part grandmother, helps young
people and restores the proper balance to life for the
Indians and the supernatural beings on the Northwest Coast.
1. Indians of North America—Northwest coast of
North America—Legends. [1. Indians of North America—
Northwest coast of North America—Legends]
I. Tait, Douglas. II. Title.
E78.N78H33   398.2   76–25846
ISBN 0–689–30554–0

Text copyright © 1977 by Christie Harris
Illustrations copyright © 1977 by Douglas Tait
Published simultaneously in Canada by
McClelland & Stewart, Ltd.
Manufactured in the United States of America by
Halliday Lithograph Corporation
West Hanover, Massachusetts
Book design by Mary M. Ahern
First Edition

TO

the native people of the Northwest Coast,
who gave us Mouse Woman

Contents

Mouse Woman
and the
Mischief-Makers

Before You Read
the Stories

IT WAS IN THE TIME of very long ago, when things were different.

Then supernatural beings roamed the seas and the vast green wilderness of the Northwest Coast. The people called them narnauks. And everyone was very, very careful not to anger the narnauks.

In those days the people lived in totem pole villages that stood with their backs to the big, snow-capped mountains. The villages were bright with the carved and painted emblems of the clans: Eagle, Raven, Bear, Wolf, Frog. . . . Always fronting on the water where the totem-crested canoes were drawn up, they edged many lonely beaches; they fringed certain bays along the rivers.

The people fished the rivers. They hunted the hills and the seas. They gathered roots and berries. They built with cedar. And when winter came, they feasted in their enormous cedar houses and settled the affairs of the people. Wearing colorful regalia, they

3

drummed and chanted and danced; they told stories.

Some of the stories were about Mouse Woman, a tiny narnauk who watched the world with her big, busy, mouse eyes. Because she was a spirit being, Mouse Woman could appear as a mouse or as the tiniest of grandmothers; or she could move about without any body. Also because she was a spirit being, she should have let any gifts be transformed into their essence, by fire, for her use. But the mouse in Mouse Woman was so strong that sometimes—if the things were woolen—she snatched them up before they were more than scorched. And her ravelly little fingers began tearing them into a lovely, loose, nesty pile of wool. It was the one improper delight of a very, very proper little being.

Mouse Woman liked everyone and everything to be proper. To her, anyone who was disturbing the proper order of the world was a mischief-maker. And being the busiest little busybody in the Place-of-Supernatural-Beings, she always did something about the mischief-makers.

What she did made the stories in this book.

1

Mouse Woman and Porcupine Hunter

Once there was a man known as Porcupine Hunter.

Every autumn, when the other hunters of his village went off to their mountain goat hunting grounds, he and his wife went off to Green Mountain, where they had four huts in four different valleys. And while he searched trees and rocks for day-snoozing porcupines, his wife stayed at the hut drying the meat and fat he had already brought her. While he smoked porcupines out of their rock dens and clubbed them and killed them, she filled bags with quills and with the black underfur and white-tipped guard hairs she sheared from the skins with her hardened mussel-shell knife.

As she worked, she dreamed of being rich and important. She dreamed of wearing a lustrous sea otter cloak and long woolen ear tassels glistening with squares of abalone mother-of-pearl. She dreamed of having a great carved cedar house and a magnificently decorated canoe. To practice being a great lady, she pierced her ears; and while she was up in the valleys where no one could see her, she wore long woolen ear tassels, like a wealthy noble. For she was very ambitious. And she had thought of a way to get the things she wanted.

Every winter she sold dried porcupine meat and tallow. Then, at spring trading, she sold dancing leggings woven from porcupine hair and trimmed with porcupine quills. Since few of the Coast women worked porcupine hair or quills, her leggings were sought after. People paid her so well for them that she would soon become rich, she thought. And then noble, she thought. For she was *very* ambitious. And her husband, who was not too bright at any time, would do exactly as she told him every autumn.

Filled with dreams of wealth and importance, she kept him hunting, hunting, hunting. As soon as he had cleared the first valley of every porcupine he could find, she urged him on to the second valley, and the third valley, and the fourth valley. The future looked bright to Porcupine Hunter's wife.

It DID NOT look so bright to the porcupines, whose only ambition was to be left alone to sleep all day and waddle around all night among the tasty trees and bushes.

If *they* had a dream up there on Green Mountain, it must have been a dream of turning someone into a quill-cushion. They didn't know who that someone was, for porcupines are nearsighted and solitary, as well as sleepy in the daytime. They are also pigeon-toed, bowlegged, slow and peaceful. But they are well armed for defence at close quarters. When threatened, they burst out into a bristle of needle-sharp quills; they whirl away from the threatener and strike him with their spiny tails. And then it is the threatener who wishes he had been left alone.

The trouble was that, with Porcupine Hunter, they never knew when they were threatened. He always sneaked up on them while they were sleeping in a tree or in a rock den. His arrow or club always struck them before they had time to bristle.

And with almost no one around but nearsighted solitary porcupines, almost no one knew what was happening. So, being porcupines, they just kept on sleeping all day and waddling around all night, nearsighted, solitary, pigeon-toed, bowlegged, slow and peaceful.

ONE WHO did know what was happening and who was hopping mad about it was Mouse Woman.

"Mischief-makers!" she squeaked again and again as she watched Porcupine Hunter and his wife with big, busy, mouse eyes. By taking more than they needed, they were upsetting the order of the world. And where would it all end? What would happen when there were no more porcupines to move into these mountain valleys? And what was the Great Porcupine going to do about it? Every time she thought about it, her nose twitched.

"He must do something about it," she squeaked to herself one day. "And it must not be something foolish."

That was a danger. For a meeting of the animals

had once voted the porcupine the wisest of all the animals and Head Chief of all the small ones. And ever since, the Great Porcupine had been a foolishly vain fellow.

"I'll pay him a visit," she told herself. And transforming herself into a white mouse, she scurried off along the trail to the fourth valley, where he now lived.

THE GREAT PORCUPINE was one narnauk who no longer cared to live in the Place-of-the-Supernatural-Beings with other narnauks. Like his porcupines, he just wanted to be left alone—especially by Mouse Woman, the busiest little busybody in the Place. So he had hidden Porcupine House under big rocks at the foot of a slope in the fourth valley on Green Mountain. And that was why so many porcupines kept moving onto that mountain, and why—until Porcupine Hunter came into their world—they had all been very happy.

The Great Porcupine liked to sleep all day and potter about all night in his human shape, wearing his porcupine Robe-of-Tails. For he, too, was nearsighted, solitary, pigeon-toed, bowlegged, slow and peaceful; and the Robe was his defender. Being a supernatural living porcupine Robe, it bristled at any threat, and struck the unwary with a score of spiny tails. For the Robe was *hung* with porcupine tails.

The Great Porcupine was as vain of his Robe as he was of his wisdom and his Head Chieftainship. The fur of the Robe was so richly black and so beautifully overlaid with white-tipped guard hairs that he could never understand why it was sea otter cloaks the humans wanted. Sea otters didn't even have quills full of piercing power. But since fellow narnauks, too, seemed to think sea otter fur more handsome than porcupine fur, he drew their attention to the basic similarity of the furs by taking the name Sea-Otter-on-Green-Mountain. A fine name for a fine fellow, he thought.

At the moment though, the Great Porcupine was scowling. He was wishing Porcupine Hunter would surprise *him* and his Robe one of these days. He was even half planning to start pottering about in the daytime while the man was hunting. He had to do something. But he did wish he could think of something worthy of the wisest of all the narnauks and Head Chief of all the small ones. Something that would add to his fame. Something that people would tell of in their feast houses.

"What am I going to do about that hunter?" he asked himself, out loud.

"I can tell you what you're not going to do," somebody answered.

He whirled so suddenly at the squeaky voice that Mouse Woman might have been turned into an indignant quill-cushion if she had not been standing at a respectful distance from the Robe-of-Tails. For she, too, was in her human form.

"You!" her Head Chief said, scowling worse than ever.

"Fortunately for you, yes," she answered, looking up at him with her big, busy, mouse eyes. "And the thing you are not going to do is carry off a human princess." Mouse Woman's nose twitched.

"Bring another human here?" he demanded, red-faced at the very mention of *another* human.

"Good!" Mouse Woman said, settling her field mouse robe on her tiny shoulders as she glanced about for any likely bits of wool. For the Chief's ears were hung with tassels of porcupine quills. And needle-sharp quills were not exactly what she wanted for her ravelly little fingers.

"But what *are* you going to do, Sea-Otter-on-Green-Mountain?" she demanded. And she wrinkled her nose at the chief's name. "A most unlikely name!" she added.

"Unlikely name?" The Chief opened his mouth to protest. Then just held his mouth open, and his near-sighted eyes brightened. His name! He could use his name to deal with that greedy hunter. For on the Northwest Coast, a great name held great power; it kept lesser people in their place, doing what they ought to be doing.

"You have a plan?" Mouse Woman asked him.

"A wise plan," he told her, drawing himself up grandly in his Robe-of-Tails. "A plan that needs no help from you, nosey Grandmother."

"We shall see," she answered.

"We *shall* see!" he retorted. "So you just disappear! Back to where you came from!"

Mouse Woman disappeared. But not back to where she came from. She had every intention of seeing that the wisest of all the narnauks did not do something foolish. "You have not seen the last of me!" her invisible self told him.

"That would be too much to hope," he answered. But his eyes were bright with planning.

IT WAS EARLY next morning when Porcupine Hunter came out of his hut with his club and his bow and arrows, ready to clear the fourth valley of the porcupines his wife wanted.

Since his wife had no animals to work on this first morning in the valley, she came out to hunt with him. Together they could seek out even more porcupines and fill even more bags.

"Where shall we start?" he asked her.

As if in answer, a large brown porcupine waddled around the base of a spruce tree and then disappeared among some big rocks at the foot of a nearby slope.

"Brown?" the hunter said. Not too bright at any time, he found a brown porcupine confusing in a land where black porcupines were the custom.

"Yes, brown!" his wife cried out. She was not a bit confused. Brown leggings would fetch a better price than black leggings. "We'll start there," she told him. And she spurted off toward the big rocks where the animal had vanished.

When they reached the rocks, a very strange thing happened. A big rock door opened. Beyond the opened door they saw the vast darkness of a house lighted by a central lodge fire. And beyond the fire they glimpsed a Chief in a dark fur robe.

Being dressed for work, they themselves wore only their small leather aprons. Porcupine Hunter just stood there in his small leather apron, with his mouth open. But his wife, furious at the thought of someone else moving into *her* valley, snapped her opened mouth shut.

"Come in!" the Chief commanded.

So they went in.

"Sit down!" the Chief invited. And his tone was so lordly that even the wife did not dare to challenge his move into *her* valley. She just sat down by the fire, on a mat placed a short distance from her husband's.

The Chief lifted a hand. And four young men emerged from the shadows of the vast house. They moved with a strangely slow waddle and then stood waiting their Chief's command with strangely sleepy faces.

The wife edged toward her husband. There was something strange about these people.

Again the Chief spoke. "Messengers! Run around the village and—"

"Village?" the hunter blurted out. He had seen no village.

"—and invite the women to my house, that I may dance to welcome my guests."

"Women?" the hunter blurted out. He had seen no women.

Yet women streamed in on silent bare feet, wearing their fringed dancing blankets. And every blanket glistened with tassels of quills, which made a dry, eerie rustle as the women moved.

"Sing!" the Chief commanded. And as someone in the vast blackness of the shadows began to tap softly on a drum, the women began to sing, shuffling slowly around the fire, in a strangely sleepy way.

The wife edged a little closer to her husband.

"Name me my name! Name me my name!" they sang. "Strike! Strike!" At each "Strike!" they whirled round like a startled porcupine and struck the air with the porcupine tail they carried. And their tassels made a dry, eerie rustle in the dark hush that followed.

"Name me my name! Name me my name! Strike! Strike!"

HUSH

"Name me my name! Name me my name! Strike! Strike!"

HUSH.

Porcupine Hunter began to look anxious, while his wife began to shiver in her small leather apron. There was something very, very strange about these people.

Then the Chief rose from his seat beyond the fire. And as the women muted their song and moved it back into a wider, more shadowed circle, he began to dance. He began to sing, too.

"Name me my name! Name me my name!" he sang. "Strike! Strike!" And at each "Strike!" he, too, whirled round like a startled porcupine; his Robe-of-Tails bristled out like a porcupine monster; and its spiny tails lashed out, just missing the two terrified human beings.

Finally the Chief stood right in front of the hunter.

"Name me my name!" he commanded. "Name me my name!"

"Your name is . . . is . . . is Porcupine Monster." The hunter blurted out the first name that struck him.

"Strike! Strike!" The offended Chief's name was

not Porcupine Monster. The hunter's face was full of quills. And the wife's face bristled with a few chance loose quills that caught her.

The Chief repeated his dance and stood once more before the hunter.

"Name me my name!" he commanded. "Name me my name!"

The hunter's wife tried it. "Your name is . . . is . . . is Big Porcupine."

"Strike! Strike!" The offended Chief's name was not Big Porcupine. The hunter's face was even more full of quills. And the wife's face bristled with even more chance loose quills that caught her.

Again the Chief repeated his dance. Again he stood before Porcupine Hunter.

"Name me my name!" he commanded. "Name me my name!"

Both humans blurted out something. Anything.

"Little Lean Fellow!"

"Little Fat Fellow!"

"Strike! Strike!" The offended Chief's name was not Little Lean Fellow nor Little Fat Fellow. And now the hunter's face was a forest of quills. The wife's face was a hodgepodge of chance loose quills that caught her. And they were both terrified. They knew that porcupine quills had scaly tips that dug into the flesh and stayed there. Instead of pulling out easily, they just kept moving on in, deeper and deeper. Already their faces were swollen. Their eyes were almost puffed shut, and partly blinded. And where would it all end?

Yes, invisible Mouse Woman thought, *where*

would it all end? The next chance at the name would be the fourth and last chance. They'd never guess such an unlikely name. The Chief would be upset to realize his unimportance in the world. And in his rage, he and his people would quill the humans to death. Then there'd be nobody to go back to the village and tell people how to treat porcupines. And when the Chief realized that, he'd be more upset than ever. And where would it all end?

He had said that his plan did not need her help.

HMPH! thought Mouse Woman. Anyway, her invisible ravelly little fingers were itching for the wife's long woolen ear tassels. So, as the Chief began to dance for the fourth and last time, she watched for her moment.

This time it was a long, long, slow waddle of a dance to give the forgetful couple plenty of time to remember an important name.

But Mouse Woman wasted no time. As soon as the Chief had waddled away, with his back toward the couple, she confronted them. A tiny, but very important person.

The hunter blinked his swollen eyes.

The wife caught her breath.

"Do you know who is punishing you?" Mouse Woman asked the astonished couple. And her eyes were watching the swing of the wife's woolen tassels.

"No!" they gasped, peering out of their swollen faces, desperate for the Chief's name.

But as always, Mouse Woman did things her own way. "Punishing you because you have killed more porcupines than you needed. For years!"

They both swallowed.

"He is the Great Porcupine, the Supernatural Chief of All Porcupines," Mouse Woman went on, in her own way. "And his people will kill you because you have killed far more porcupines than you ever needed." She touched one woolen tassel and set it swinging.

They swallowed again. And they kept glancing anxiously at the slow, stately, waddly dancer.

"Throw your ear ornaments in the fire!" Mouse Woman commanded. For if help were to be given, something must be given in return. That was the great law that kept everything equal.

The wife snatched them from her ears and hurled them at the fire.

But before they were more than scorched, Mouse Woman spirited them out. And her ravelly little fingers began tearing them into a lovely, loose, nesty pile of mountain goat wool. Then, having received her favorite gift, she properly proceeded to give, in return, her favorite giving—advice to someone in trouble.

"Tell him his name is Sea-Otter-on-Green-Mountain," she advised them. And she was gone, like a breath of wind, before the Great Porcupine saw her.

The dancer made one more whirl, one more waddle. Then he stood once more before the hunter.

"Name me my name!" he commanded, for the fourth and last time. "Name me my name!"

They both blurted it out. "SEA-OTTER-ON-GREEN-MOUNTAIN!"

"Yes . . . that is my name." The Chief looked

surprised and relieved and boastful, all at once. People *did* know his great name. And they *would* tell his story in all the feast houses. They would tell it just as he, the Great Wise One, had planned.

"Not unless they live to tell it," an invisible voice squeaked in his right ear.

"Of course," he agreed, making a swipe at his ear. He didn't need HER to tell him that he must cure his victims for the storytelling. A wave of his hand summoned the women, who began to treat the bristling faces with the contents of porcupines' stomachs. Again and again they treated the bristling faces. And the quills began to drop out.

Porcupine Hunter and his wife sagged with relief. But their faces were still swollen and full of red scars.

"Hm," the Chief said, considering the effect of their return to the village with their porcupine story. He chewed vigorously on certain green leaves he took from a box. Then he rubbed the chewed leaves on his hands. And finally he rubbed his hands over the hunter's face. And a very strange thing happened.

Under his hands, the man's face became as clear and as smooth as a boy's face. His eyes became as bright and as eager as a boy's eyes. He became a beautiful young man.

The wife's mouth dropped open at the transformation. And she moved closer to the Chief, for her turn.

But the Great Porcupine ignored her.

"Now you will go back to your village," he commanded the hunter. "You will give a great feast with all the meat and fat you have taken from my other valleys. And you will tell the people what has happened in the house of Sea-Otter-on-Green-Mountain. You will tell them that people must take only what they *need*."

The hunter nodded, as eagerly as a boy. He would do exactly as the Chief commanded.

His wife peered out of her swollen, scarred face, still hoping for her turn. But the Great Porcupine still ignored her.

"And you will tell the people how we have healed you," the Chief went on. "So they will know how to remove porcupine quills. For we are a peaceful people who wish to harm no one."

Again the hunter nodded, as eagerly as a boy. He would do exactly as the Chief told him.

"Now you will go!"

Porcupine Hunter nodded once more and bounded toward the door.

Swallowing her disappointment, his wife followed him with her swollen, scarred face. She knew he would do exactly as the Chief had told him. And her dreams would come to nothing.

The moment they were gone, Mouse Woman appeared. She did a merry little porcupine dance around the fire. "Name me my name!" she squeaked. "Name me my name! Strike! Strike!"

She stopped before the Great Porcupine.

"YOU again!" He scowled down at the little busybody. Then he began to smile. "It's good you have come after all, nosey Grandmother," he told her. "It's good for you to see for yourself that the people did know my great name. Unlikely name, indeed! And it's good for you to see for yourself that my plan did not need your help." He drew himself up grandly in his Robe-of-Tails. For now that he had dealt with the greedy humans, *in his wisdom*, he and his porcupines could go back to sleeping all day and waddling around all night, nearsighted, solitary, pigeon-toed, bowlegged, slow and peaceful.

"It's good for me to see for myself," Mouse Woman agreed. Then she flashed a sly glance up at Sea-Otter-on-Green-Mountain. She bustled over to where the two humans had sat. And she picked up her pile of lovely, loose, nesty mountain goat wool.

Now *his* mouth dropped open. Making the wisest of all the narnauks look very, very foolish.

And that was strangely satisfying to tiny Mouse Woman.

2

Mouse Woman and the Vanished Princes

ONCE THERE WERE mischief-makers who didn't mean to be mischief-makers. Yet they caused many youths to vanish from a certain village at the mouth of a river.

Since these mischief-makers-who-didn't-mean-to-be-mischief-makers belonged to the Mouse People, Mouse Woman was most concerned. And to see what she could do about it, the tiny narnauk spirited her house to the side of a faint trail that ran upriver from the village.

The reason the trail was faint was that most of the people in the village were afraid to travel on it. They knew that strange beings lived upriver. Only the most daring—or the most foolish—boys ventured along the trail. And these were the ones who vanished.

Now IN THIS VILLAGE lived a high-ranking Eagle woman who had ten children: nine sons and a daughter, all living with her.

It was the proper custom, of course, for such noble boys to live with the maternal uncle, whose duty it was to train them in the skills and virtues expected of them. But sometimes people grew careless of custom. To Mouse Woman's annoyance.

"No good ever comes of upsetting the proper order of the world," she muttered every time she thought of this family. "No good will come of it now."

And so it seemed. For one by one, as they grew up, the Eagle princes yearned to venture along the faint trail. One by one, they listened eagerly to the rumors of a wonderful place where the sun was always shining, the flowers were always blooming, the birds were always singing, and people stayed young forever. One by one, they listened even more eagerly to the rumors of the mysterious maidens who lived there—maidens who were as beautiful as the wild roses and as graceful as the swallows.

When her eldest son became a youth, the mother saw the faraway look in his eyes. And she knew he was dreaming of the mysterious maidens.

"Those maidens have a terrible power," she warned him. For it was rumored that if a youth angered one of them, she laid a spell on him, turning him into a stump from the waist down.

"Maidens?" the son protested, as if it were not they who filled his dreams. "Mother, I want to see the wonderful house of their Chief-woman." It was said to be a glistening blue-green house by a lake; the glisten was the iridescent sheen of abalone mother-of-pearl. And sometimes the Chief-woman went out on the lake in a glistening blue-green canoe.

"I want to see that canoe," the youth told his mother.

"On that lake?" his mother gasped. For it was well known that the terrible Wasco often went to that lake. The reason, people said, was that it had a taste for the tender youths who were lured there by their dreams of the mysterious maidens.

Now the Wasco was a monster that usually lived in the sea. But it could travel on land as well as in the water. It had the head and body of a wolf, with the fins of a killer whale. And though it was often wolf size, it could make itself large enough to carry three killer whales. There were awesome carvings of the Wasco with a killer whale in its teeth, another between its two ears, and yet another on its back, under the forward curl of its monstrous wolf tail. People said the Wasco's power was in its skin. If a man could overcome the Wasco, they said, and take its skin as a supernatural blanket, then he would be able to catch whales as easily as the Wasco did.

Of course, the mother reminded her son, the Wasco was not the only monster a youth might encounter on his way to the Place where the sun was always shining, the flowers were always blooming, the birds were always singing, and people stayed young forever. There was also the monster who lived in the House-of-Ice-That-Never-Melts at the head of the river. He had the power to send boulders crashing down the valley when youths ventured along the trail. He had the power to topple a great swath of trees toward them, to send them racing back to where they came from.

"Mother, I can protect myself," the youth assured her. And to prove that he could, he dropped a sea gull with a swift arrow; he stopped a mouse with a swift stone-and-cord that strangled the tiny creature.

Alarm shadowed his mother's eyes. For clearly her son was so intent on the skills he might need on his journey that he failed in his respect for living creatures.

She would have been even more alarmed if she had known that the mysterious maidens were really Mouse People who sometimes scurried around the place as tiny field mice.

But she did not know. And it was just as well. For all her warnings fell on deaf ears. Her eldest son followed the faint trail that ran upriver from the village. And he never came back.

The Eagle prince had vanished. And his mother was full of sorrow.

Then, when her second son became a youth, the high-ranking Eagle woman saw the faraway look in his eyes. And she knew that he, too, was dreaming of the mysterious maidens.

"Those maidens have a terrible power," she warned him.

"I want to see the wonderful blue-green house and the glistening canoe of their Chief-woman," he told her.

"On that lake?" his mother gasped. "The Wasco goes to that lake, and it has a taste for tender youths who are lured there by a dream of the mysterious maidens."

But, again, her warnings fell on deaf ears.

"Then there is the monster who sends boulders crashing down the valley and topples great swaths of trees," she added.

"Mother, I can protect myself," the youth assured her. And to prove that he could, he dropped a song-bird with a swift arrow; he stopped a squirrel with a swift stone-and-cord that strangled the tiny creature.

As before, alarm shadowed the mother's eyes. For clearly this son, too, was so intent on the skills he might need for his journey that he failed in his respect for living creatures.

And her fears were well founded, for her second son soon followed the faint trail that ran upriver from the village. And he never came back.

The Eagle prince had vanished. And his mother was full of sorrow.

And so it went, year after year. One by one, as they grew up, six other sons yearned to venture along the faint trail to the place where the sun was always shining, the flowers were always blooming, the birds were always singing, and people stayed young forever. As before, her warnings fell on deaf ears. One by one, six more sons followed the faint trail that ran upriver from the village. And they never came back.

Now eight Eagle princes had vanished. And their mother was lost in sorrow. She had only one son left, with her daughter. And he was small comfort to her.

Instead of doing things to gladden her heart or to fill the food boxes, her only remaining son just fasted and sought visions while he grew weaker and weaker. Soon he, too, would be gone, she told her daughter. And then it was the daughter who was full of sorrow.

For she loved her youngest brother dearly.

She knew that he fasted and sought visions. She knew, too, that he was trying to gain mighty spirit power. And she knew why.

It was to overcome the Wasco, that clearly had devoured his eight brothers. For such a test he needed mighty spirit power. After all, what was a youth's strength against a monster's?

Yet he needed a youth's strength, too. And one day he began to strive for it.

His sister was glad to help him. There was strength for him in the sea, she knew. But the northern sea was too cold for a youth who was almost too weak to walk. So day after day she put salt water into an old canoe, and the youth bathed there.

Eventually, when he felt strong enough, he began to swim in the sea. Day after day after day he swam, until a wise and watching old man said, "You will be turning into a Wasco." When he caught the flash in the youth's eyes at mention of the monster, he knew what the Eagle prince was planning. And he, too, began to help him. Each time the youth came out of the sea, the old man rubbed him with green boughs until his skin flamed like a sunrise. And day after day after day, the youth grew stronger.

He sought strength from the trees of the forest, also; for there was great power in the trees. Running along the trails, he would stop and ask a tree to help him. "Wrestle with me, friend," he would ask the tree. And then he would twist a strong tree bough against the tree's strength, until his own strength was enough to wrench it from its socket. And day after day after day, he felt the power of the great trees surging through his body.

His mother's eyes brightened as she saw her weak son regaining his proper strength. Then her eyes shadowed. For she glimpsed the faraway look in this son's eyes, too. Was her only remaining son dreaming of the mysterious maidens?

She might have been even more alarmed if she had known that he was dreaming of the monster that could carry a killer whale in its teeth, another between its two ears, and yet another on its back under the forward curl of its monstrous wolf tail.

But she did not know. And if she had, her warnings would have fallen on deaf ears. One day her only remaining son followed the faint trail that ran upriver from the village. And she felt that he, too, would never come back. The Wasco would devour him as it had his brothers.

THE EAGLE PRINCE had not gone far along the trail before he heard a terrible noise upriver. It was the sound of boulders crashing, and soon he saw great boulders rushing and bouncing and clattering toward him. So he hurried into the woods.

But a terrible noise began there, too. It was the sound of trees cracking and crashing, and then he saw a great swath of trees toppling toward him. With this there seemed to be a voice calling to him, "GO BACK! GO BACK!"

But another voice called to him: "HELP ME! HELP ME! HELP ME!" It seemed to come from a clump of bushes on the river bank. There he saw a youth's head above the bushes, and a youth's arms flailing wildly at him. So he raced that way. And a very strange thing happened. The boulders stopped rushing and bouncing and clattering toward him. The trees stopped crackling and crashing and toppling toward him.

When he reached the youth, he saw a fearsome thing. The slender youth was a slender stump from the waist down. A spell had been laid on him.

"The spell of the mysterious maidens!" the Eagle prince muttered, aghast at what had happened to this youth and what might have happened to his own brothers.

"Help me! Help me!" the youth begged.

So the Eagle prince put his arms around the slender stump and pulled with all the power he had gained from his spirit visions and with all the strength he had gained from the sea and from the trees of the forest. And the slender stump came out in his arms.

At once the youth regained his former shape. He glanced gratefully at his rescuer, but fearfully upriver. "Beware of the field mice!" he warned. Then, terrified of venturing nearer to the Place where the sun was always shining, the flowers were always blooming, the birds were always singing, and people stayed young forever, he raced back along the faint trail to the shelter of the village.

"Beware of the field mice?" the Eagle prince muttered, looking after the fleeing youth. For he did not yet know that to harm a field mouse here was to harm a mysterious maiden and receive a terrible spell of enchantment.

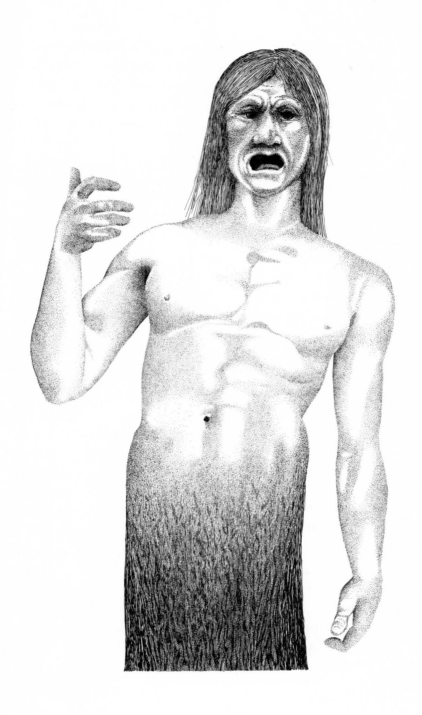

He went on his way, but he had gone far when he encountered a field mouse. A lame field mouse. It was having trouble trying to climb over a big log.

"Let me help you, little friend," the prince said. And he gently lifted the little lame mouse over the big log. He watched it with compassionate eyes as it vanished into a thicket of large ferns.

Then a very strange thing happened. A voice called to him from behind the thicket of large ferns. "Come in!" it invited. And though the voice was small and squeaky, it was the voice of a Chief-woman. "Come in!" it commanded the Eagle prince.

The astonished youth parted the ferns and became even more astonished. For there was a house decorated all over with Mouse totems.

"Come in, my dear!" the imperious squeak commanded.

So he went in. And there was the tiniest grandmother he had ever seen. She had a field mouse robe on her tiny shoulders. And she was watching him with her big, busy, mouse eyes.

"Mouse Woman!" he cried out. Then he hushed himself with awe, for Mouse Woman was a narnauk. But his eyes still shone. For everyone knew that Mouse Woman was a friend to young people. He put his hand to his long woolen hair ornament. For everyone also knew that Mouse Woman liked wool for her ravelly little fingers.

But this time she shook her head in refusal of his gift. "You have already given me service," she told him, though her fingers *were* itching. "And besides . . ."

And besides, she did not bother to explain, *it was her relatives—Mouse People—who had lured his brothers to the place where the Wasco had devoured them. However innocently, her relatives had helped deprive him of his brothers. So the maidens' relatives must compensate the brothers' relatives for their loss. That was a sacred law on the Northwest Coast. Clearly it was the only way to keep things equal.*

Still . . . she told herself, looking longingly at the tassel, his brothers had brought their troubles on themselves. Her nose twitched at the very thought of those unkind princes. Then it twitched again at the thought of getting her ravelly little fingers into that lovely, long woolen hair tassel. But she turned her eyes from it. She would do what she could for him, in compensation. That was only proper.

"First, my dear, I will give you food. For you are very, very hungry, and you have strong work to do."

He was very, very, very hungry. And very, very surprised at what she handed as food to a youth who had strong work to do.

"*I'm* not a field mouse," he thought, looking at the small piece of salmon in the small bowl.

"Eat as much as you wish, my dear!" Mouse Woman invited.

"Yes, Grandmother," he said as gratefully as he could. He ate the small piece of salmon. And a strange thing happened. There was another small piece of salmon in the small bowl. And then another, and another. As long as he ate, there was more to be eaten. And Mouse Woman kept her ravelly little fingers firmly under her field mouse robe while she kept her big, busy, mouse eyes firmly off his long woolen hair tassel. But her nose twitched.

By and by she gave him another small bowl.

"*I'm* not a field mouse," he thought as he looked at the one cranberry in the small bowl.

"Eat as much as you wish, my dear!" Mouse Woman invited.

"Yes, Grandmother," he said as gratefully as he could. He ate the one cranberry, and there was another cranberry in the small bowl. And then another, and another. As long as he ate, there was more to be eaten. And Mouse Woman kept her ravelly little fingers firmly under her field mouse robe while she kept her big, busy, mouse eyes firmly off his long woolen hair tassel. But her nose did twitch. Very often!

"And now, my dear," the tiny narnauk said, "it has come to my ears that you need to borrow something from me."

The Eagle prince opened his mouth in surprise. It had not come to *his* ears that he needed to borrow something from her.

Mouse Woman bustled over to a corner of her house and opened a carved box. She took out a tray that was edged with tiny mouse figures and handed the Eagle prince what looked like a small square of whale blubber. Only it was as blue as a mountain lake.

"Chew this when you think you need power," she told him. "And rub the juice on yourself or spit it onto whatever you need to spit it onto." That was all she told him.

"Yes, Grandmother," the youth said gratefully. And he put the blubber carefully into a leather pouch he carried at his waist. Then, catching her longing glance at his hair, he pulled off the long woolen tassel and tossed it on the fire.

Before it was more than scorched, Mouse Woman spirited it out of the fire, and her ravelly little fingers began tearing it into a lovely, loose, nesty pile of mountain sheep wool. Clearly this was very satisfying to the tiniest of the narnauks.

THE EAGLE PRINCE went on his way, always watching for stump-men. It was possible that his brothers could have angered the mysterious maidens and come under their fearsome enchantment. But though he found several such enchanted youths and released them from the spell, they were not his brothers. Clearly it was the Wasco that had taken his brothers.

At last he came to the Place. And the sun *was* shining. The flowers were blooming. The birds were singing. And clearly people stayed young forever. For he saw only beautiful maidens flitting through the woods.

But his mind was on the Wasco. His eyes were searching for the monster with the head and body of a wolf and the fins of a killer whale.

He saw the blue-green canoe, and the blue-green house glistening by a lake. And the glisten *was* the iridescent sheen of abalone mother-of-pearl.

But his mind was on the Wasco. Nothing seemed to be moving in the lake. Its clear waters were as calm and as still as a tidal pool in summer.

Then he heard a fearsome sound. It was like the howl of a wolf, yet like the screaming whistle of a killer whale, too.

Trembling with sudden terror, the Eagle prince chewed the blue blubber and rubbed the juice on himself to take away his human scent before he raced into the woods. He hid in a tree to see what he would see, though it was rumored that the Wasco, too, could climb trees.

Very soon he saw it coming. And truly it was a fearsome sight. As big as a large wolf, it had the fins of a killer whale and eyes that glowed red as live coals. Though it moved in the shallow water by the river bank, it kept sniffing the land. Clearly it had caught the scent of a tender youth. And the Wasco had a taste for tender youths.

It sniffed and snuffled its way to the very spot where he had chewed the blue blubber. Then, howling and whistling with rage at the loss of the human scent, it splashed into the lake. And making itself big enough to have carried three killer whales, it churned the still waters into a red foam.

The Eagle prince swallowed his terror and watched until the fearsome monster came, at last, out of the lake, once more the size of a large wolf. Again it sniffed and snuffled its way to the very spot where he had chewed the blue blubber. Then with a howl and whistle of rage, it loped back downriver, again moving in the shallow water close to the river bank.

It would come back. He knew it would come back. But how soon? He did not know. But whenever it came, he must be ready for it. He must make a trap to catch the Wasco. And he must bait the trap with a strong scent of a tender youth.

Almost stumbling with the need for haste, he made his way downriver until he found a tree close to the bank—a tree tall enough to span the narrow river. He must fell it across an old log lying between it and the river so that the trunk would be high enough above the water for his purpose.

When he had felled the tree across the log and across the river, he spliced strong supple boughs together to make several nooses, which he hung from the fallen tree. On each he spat the wonderful blue juice, to give them power to hold the monster. And as he worked in desperate haste, he kept listening for the fearsome sound that was like the howl of a wolf, yet like the screaming whistle of a killer whale, too.

At last the trap was ready. And all around it was the scent of a tender youth. Then, once more, the Eagle prince chewed the blue blubber, rubbed the wonderful juice on himself, and raced into the woods to hide in a tree.

He dared not leave his tree to find food. He dared not go to sleep when night came. And it was the next afternoon before he heard the fearsome sound. Again it was like the howl of a wolf, yet like the screaming whistle of a killer whale, too.

Then he saw it coming. And he clung to his tree in terror as he watched it sniff and snuffle its way upriver to the spot where the human scent was strongest. He held his breath. For what if his nooses could not hold the supernatural?

The Wasco sniffed and snuffled ravenously as it

neared the fallen tree. And the prince scarcely dared
to let his breath out.

Suddenly, with an ear-splitting howl and whistle,
the monster lunged forward. And a noose tightened
around its throat.

But would the noose hold?

Now the Eagle prince really trembled as he
dropped to the ground. He really chewed the blue
blubber and rubbed the juice on himself, as he
stumbled to the river bank.

The strangling Wasco saw him. It lunged at him.
But the lunge tightened the noose around its throat.
Its eyes glowed red as live coals as it glared at him.
Then they closed.

The youth ventured near enough to spit the blue
juice on the strangled Wasco.

It threshed about once more, turning the shallow
water of the river into a red foam.

He spat again.

The Wasco lay still.

And now, desperate with haste and trembling with
terror, he plunged his hunting knife into the monster's soft underbelly. As he sliced along the belly, a
pile of bones fell out.

The bones of his eight brothers! He knew these
were the bones of the vanished Eagle princes. So he
tossed them onto the river bank; he chewed once
more on the blue blubber and spat the juice over the
bones.

And a wonderful thing happened.

The bones clattered themselves into place. And
suddenly, there before him stood eight Eagle princes.

All of them had come back to life. And all of them clearly felt a terror of the Place. Scarcely waiting to speak words of gratitude to their rescuer, they raced back down the faint trail to the shelter of the village.

The youngest of the Eagle princes did not race after them. Instead, he spat the blue juice on his knife and skinned the Wasco. For the power of the Wasco was in its skin, which would live forever. And it was rumored that if a man could overcome the Wasco and take its skin as a supernatural blanket, then he would be able to catch whales as easily as the Wasco caught them.

When all was accomplished, he took the blue blubber back to Mouse Woman, who had used the word "borrow."

But this time she gave it to him. For he had proved himself worthy of supernatural aid. And she knew that he would need the blue power often. She knew he was destined to venture out into the sea many times in the living skin of the Wasco. As a great sea hunter with the Wasco for his personal crest, he was destined to win the great name of Whale Catcher.

When he had gone off to start his marvelous adventures, Mouse Woman did a merry little mouse dance. For those who had been deprived had been compensated. And it was all very satisfying.

Then, too, the Wasco, who had upset the order of the world by having tender youths inside him, now had more youth than he had ever wanted inside his living skin.

And the eight vanished princes?

Mouse Woman stopped dancing. She frowned.

And her nose twitched. For she knew that they would be tempted again by the mysterious maidens. They would have to be rescued again by their more valiant brother. And perhaps it was all because they had not been taken properly in hand by the uncles whose duty it was to train them in the skills and virtues expected of them.

"No good ever comes of upsetting the proper order of the world," she muttered.

Then she bustled away from the Place where the sun was always shining, the flowers were always blooming, the birds were always singing, and people stayed young forever.

3

Mouse Woman and the Snee-nee-iq

ONCE THERE WAS a narnauk who was upsetting the order of Mouse Woman's world, by tricking children into trouble.

It was in the time of very long ago, when things were different. Then, supernatural beings called narnauks roamed the vast green wildernesses of the Northwest. Some of them were helpful to human beings. There was Song Woman, who flew over lonely places with songs coming from every part of her, like a flock of songbirds. She threw songs into worthy people, to give them something to sing in the feast houses. And there was the invisible Father-of-All-Mountain-Goats, who roamed the hills with only his hunting hat and his mountain staff showing. He helped hunters. And then, of course, there was Mouse Woman, who watched the world with her big, busy, mouse eyes and helped people who'd been tricked into trouble.

But there were also narnauks who were harmful to

human beings. There was Great-Whirlpool-Maker, who released a terrible whirling power that could suck down even the greatest of the great northern canoes as if it were nothing but a bit of driftwood. And there was the Snee-NEE-iq, who carried off children to her mountain hut and ate them. She carried them off in a big basket slung on her back by a tumpline around her forehead.

It was the Snee-nee-iq who was now upsetting the order of Mouse Woman's world.

"It's time somebody did something about her," the tiny narnauk told herself. And since the Snee-nee-iq lived faraway along the South Trail, she bustled off along the South Trail.

"That's no way to treat any child," she kept squeaking to herself as she went along.

But there was one child she didn't yet know about —a child who also was upsetting the order of the world.

This child was a girl who lived in a village at the foot of the Snee-nee-iq's mountain. A most annoying child! She howled for everything she wanted. And she wanted everything just when it wasn't handy.

Now she wanted mountain goat tallow. Just when all the food had been put away and the people had gone to sleep in the big cedar house at the foot of the mountain.

"I want mountain goat tallow!" the child screeched.

"No!" her mother told her.

"Then I shall cry all night." And to prove it, the girl started howling and howling.

"If you don't stop crying, I shall turn you out of the house," her mother warned. "And then the Snee-nee-iq will get you."

"I hope she does!" The girl kept on howling and howling.

"I hope she does!" grown-ups echoed from their sleeping platforms. While the children, rudely wakened from their sleep, whispered, "Snee-nee-iq?" And as they snuggled down deeper into their rabbit skin blankets, they seemed to hear a voice in the wind, calling, "Sneeeee-neeeee-iq! Sneeeee-neeeee-iq!" For all the children feared her.

All except the one child.

"I don't believe she eats children!" she screeched. And she went right on howling and howling, though she was getting a little weary.

Then, suddenly, she too seemed to hear a voice in the wind, calling to her.

"Commmmmmme with meeeeee, my deaaaaaaar. I willlllllll give youuuuuuuuu mountain goat tallowwwwwwwww," the voice said.

The girl stopped howling to listen.

"Commmmmmmmmme with meeeeee, my deaaaaar. I willlllll give youuuuuuuuu mountain goat tallowwwwwwww."

"I'm going out of the house!" the girl screeched. "So I'll get what I desire."

"So you'll get what you deserve," grown-ups muttered from their sleeping platforms. While the children just snuggled down deeper into their rabbit skin blankets and tried to shut their ears to the voice in the wind, calling, calling. . . .

"And you'll be sorry!" the girl shouted, as she flounced out of the house.

But nobody sounded sorry. They all just went back to sleep in the big cedar house at the foot of the mountain.

Outside, there was pale light, as there is in the northern summer nights. Then a shadow fell on the girl. And there stood the biggest woman she had ever seen. But before she could do more than gasp, the woman spoke to her kindly. "Come with me, my dear. And I will give you mountain goat tallow."

"I intend to go with you," the girl said. For she did not believe the Snee-nee-iq ate children. It was just something mothers told you to keep you quiet. But she did pull her rabbit skin robe more tightly around her shoulders. She did glance about her, at the long black shadows. And she did steal a few anxious peeks at the giantess as they started up the mountain. For the woman was truly enormous.

It was dark in the forest, with the silent trees crowding in on the girl, catching at her hair. The trail twisted up through drooping cedars and brooding firs in a world hushed by deep, deep, dark mosses. Only pale owls flitted across the trail, like ghosts; and like ghosts they made no sound in passing.

The girl didn't like it. But scrambling up the steep mountain behind the huge giantess, she had no breath left for complaints. Well, almost no breath. "I'm tired!" she finally burst out. "I . . . don't . . . think . . . I'll go . . . with you." And she stopped where she was to look back along the dark, silent trail.

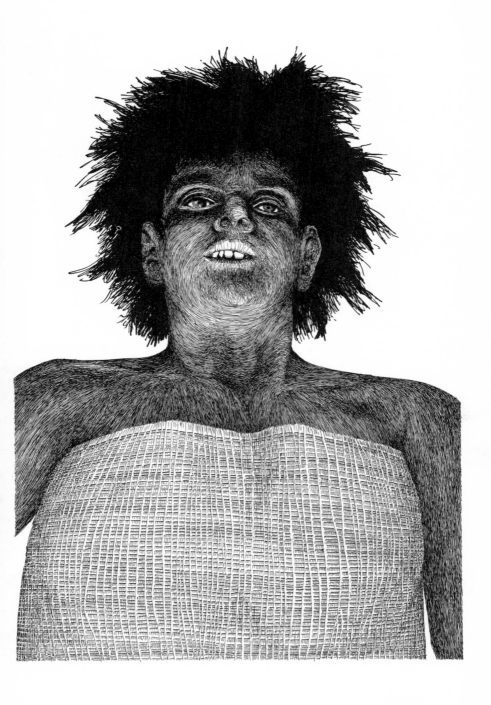

"Oh, let me carry you in my basket, my dear," the woman said kindly. Her hands were as quick and as hard as fire tongs as she picked up the girl and dropped her into the basket.

It was deep inside, like a dark well. And the basket thudded against the Snee-nee-iq's back as she thudded up the mountain. On and on and on and on up the mountain..

"I don't like it in here!" the girl screeched.

But the giantess didn't seem to hear her. For she just thudded on and on and on and on up the mountain.

Then she stopped. The basket thudded on the ground. And the girl was lifted out. They had reached the Snee-nee-iq's hut.

The hut loomed black as a cave as the two went inside. Acrid smoke rose from the ashes of a fire that smouldered in the center.

The giantess lighted a torch near the door.

"I want mountain goat tallow," the girl said. She also wanted her own house. Why had her mother let her leave it?

"You shall have mountain goat tallow, my dear," the woman said kindly. "But all in good time. First I shall give you some nice, fresh, juicy berries." And she picked up a basket.

"But I want mountain goat tallow."

"After the berries, my dear," the woman said kindly. And she went out with the basket to pick berries in the pale summer night.

"I want mountain goat tallow," the girl screeched after her. But with no one else around to hear, she didn't bother to start howling. Instead, she looked about her. And . . . she gasped.

She was not alone. Back in the shadows stood several small women. They didn't move. They didn't speak. They just stood there and watched her with strangely dull eyes.

The girl pulled her rabbit skin robe about her. And she swallowed. She hoped they were sorry, back there in the big cedar house at the foot of the mountain.

Then she felt a tug at her robe. And there stood the tiniest grandmother she had ever seen. Unlike the others, the grandmother moved and twitched and wrinkled her nose. And she spoke.

"Do you know who has brought you to her house?"

"Of course I do. The Snee-nee-iq." She knew this must be Mouse Woman. But she hadn't realized that Mouse Woman was so LITTLE. "The Snee-nee-iq. But she won't eat me. . . . She . . . won't . . . eat . . . me." It was almost, but not quite, a question. "She won't eat me."

"Not unless you give her power over you," Mouse Woman agreed. For, of course, it was Mouse Woman. And her big, busy, mouse eyes were coveting the long woolen tassels the girl had not bothered to take from her braids when she had gone to bed.

"Power?" the girl asked. For clearly anybody as big as the Snee-nee-iq *had* power. "She's BIG," she reminded the tiny narnauk.

"What has size to do with anything?" Mouse Woman demanded, drawing herself up to her tiny height. And her nose twitched. "Power is what matters. And she has gone to get some."

"She's gone to get some BERRIES."

"Berries you must not eat, my dear."

"Why . . . not?"

"I'll tell you why not, my dear." But not before things were properly arranged. For Mouse Woman was a stickler for proper behavior. If she was to give advice, the girl must give something in return. "Throw your hair ornaments in the fire!"

The girl opened her mouth to protest. She liked her hair tassels. But catching the flash in the big, busy, mouse eyes, she pulled them from her tousled braids and flung them on the fire.

Before they were more than scorched, Mouse Woman spirited them out, and her ravelly little fingers began tearing them into a lovely, loose, nesty pile of mountain sheep wool. And then, having received her favorite gift, she properly proceeded to give, in return, her favorite giving—advice to a young person in trouble.

"You must not eat the berries, my dear, because they are not real berries. They are supernatural insects that will give the Snee-nee-iq power over you. The moment you eat them, they will root you to the floor." She waved a tiny hand toward the small women rooted where they stood back in the shadows. "You will be rooted to the floor until she's ready to eat you."

"Then . . . she does . . . eat children?" the girl stammered. And at last she was scared enough to speak softly.

"Only children who have let her gain power over them. So do not eat the berries!"

"But—"

But Mouse Woman had vanished. Only the still, silent women watched from the shadows with their strangely dull eyes.

The giantess thudded back into the hut.

"Here are your nice, fresh, juicy berries, my dear," she said kindly. And she gave the girl the basket.

"But . . . I want mountain goat tallow," the girl protested. And she flung the basket on the fire. The berries spilled out and scurried away in all directions. For, as Mouse Woman had warned, they were not real berries.

The Snee-nee-iq glared at the child. Just for an instant. Then she smiled. "Very well, my dear," she said kindly. "You shall have mountain goat tallow." And she thudded out of the hut with another basket.

As soon as she had gone, the girl felt a tug at her robe. And there, once more, stood the tiny narnauk.

"It will not be mountain goat tallow," Mouse Woman warned. "It will be the grease of dead people. And the moment you have eaten it, she will have you in her power."

The girl shuddered. And now she really pulled her rabbit skin robe more tightly about her shoulders. The woman might *make* her eat it. "She's . . . so . . . BIG!" she whispered.

"What has size to do with anything?" Mouse Woman demanded. And once more she drew herself up to her tiny height. "Say you are too lonely to eat," she advised the girl. "Then she will go off to fetch your little sister."

"But—"

But Mouse Woman had vanished. Only the still, silent women watched from the shadows with their strangely dull eyes.

The giantess thudded back into the hut.

"Here is your mountain goat tallow, my dear," she said kindly. And she handed the basket to the terrified child.

"I'm . . . I'm too lonely to eat," the girl screeched as loudly as she could now screech. And she flung the basket on the fire.

The giantess glared at her. Just for an instant. Then she smiled. "Very well, my dear," she said kindly. "I shall fetch you a playmate. I shall go and fetch your little sister." And she thudded away to do it.

Now the girl did not have any trouble howling and howling and howling and howling. For now she *and* her little sister would be eaten. And they would all say it was *her* fault.

"You won't be eaten unless she gains power over you with one of her evil spells," Mouse Woman squeaked, tugging at the girl's robe to stop the howling. "And before she can do that perhaps *you* can gain power over *her*. With one of her own spells!" The big, busy, mouse eyes twinkled. For it was very satisfying to use spells against their owners. Somehow, it made everything equal.

The girl stopped her howling. She opened her mouth to ask a question. But before she could ask it, she thought again about her little sister, and the way they would blame her for everything.

"Perhaps your little sister will not be carried off," Mouse Woman comforted her. "It is foolish children who bring trouble on themselves."

The girl clamped her mouth shut. Then, to turn the conversation away from children who brought trouble on themselves, she cried out, "*Can* we use one of the Snee-nee-iq's own spells against her? . . . Grandmother?"

"Time will tell," answered Mouse Woman, briskly. "And time is flying." She pointed toward a corner. "Fetch me the horns you will find in that corner!"

"That . . . corner?" the girl protested. That corner was black with shadows and . . . and . . . who knew what else? But catching a flash in the big, busy, mouse eyes, she crept fearfully toward it. And as the still, silent women watched from the shadows with their strangely dull eyes, she picked up a basket of horns.

They were black horns. Mountain goat horns. And there were ten of them. The girl took them to Mouse Woman, moving much faster on her way back to the tiny narnauk.

"Now fit a horn on each of your fingers!" Mouse Woman ordered. "And fix them firmly!"

The girl opened her mouth to protest, out of habit. But catching a flash in the big, busy, mouse eyes, she fitted the ten black horns firmly on her thumbs and fingers. "*Can* we use one of the Snee-nee-iq's own spells against her? . . . Grandmother?" she added, remembering her manners. For it was well known that Mouse Woman was a stickler for manners; and

Mouse Woman was her only friend up on this mountain.

"Time will tell. Now, when the Snee-nee-iq comes back, you will point your fingers at her, opening and closing your hands. And as you open and close your hands, you will sing, 'Yi yi yi! Open your eyes! Close your eyes! And fall down!' "

"Yi yi yi," the girl began, opening and closing her hands.

"Don't point them at me!" Mouse Woman squeaked.

The girl pointed them at a shadowed corner of the hut and began again. "Yi yi yi! Open your eyes! Close your eyes! And fall down!" She practiced and practiced and practiced. Then she flopped down and closed her eyes.

"You must not go to sleep, my dear," Mouse Woman warned. "Or the Snee-nee-iq may surprise us." And to be sure this did not happen, she tugged at the girl's robe every time she began to look sleepy. And every time, the girl scowled, out of habit. Then she swallowed, out of terror.

They went outside at dawn. And they both peered down the mountain as the morning brightened.

"There she is!" Mouse Woman squeaked. Her big, busy, mouse eyes peered down the mountain. "And her basket is empty."

"Yi yi yi!" the girl began to sing, opening and closing her hands.

"Not yet!" Mouse Woman squeaked. "You must wait until she is halfway up that final slope."

As the girl waited, terror seized her. What if her

voice froze in her throat? What if the spell did not work through *her* fingers?

Somehow, she waited until the Snee-nee-iq was halfway up the final steep slope. Then she pointed the horns at the giantess. "Yi yi yi!" she sang, as loudly as she could screech. "Open your eyes! Close your eyes! And fall down!"

But nothing happened. The Snee-nee-iq just kept thudding on up the steep slope. The stupid spell was not working.

"Yi yi yi! Open your eyes! Close your eyes! And fall down!" Now the song was a screech that did reach the big ears.

"Don't do that! Don't do that!" the giantess thundered. "If I fall down, you will never be able to get down the mountain."

"Don't listen!" Mouse Woman warned. "Just keep on singing!"

And somehow the girl did. "Yi yi yi!" she screeched, louder than she had ever screeched in the big cedar house at the foot of the mountain. "Open your eyes! Close your eyes! And fall down!"

Still nothing happened. Three times she had tried to work the spell. And nothing had happened. The Snee-nee-iq was going to eat her.

But not if she could help it.

"Yi yi yi!" she screeched for the fourth time. "Open your eyes! Close your eyes! And fall down!"

And this time the Snee-nee-iq did fall down. Down, down, down, down the final steep slope, tumbling over and over until she lay like a log at the bottom.

"I've killed her," the girl gasped.

"No, you have not killed her," Mouse Woman answered. "For humans can never kill the supernatural. Such creatures as she cannot be killed, they can only be transformed. And only fire can work the transformation. Now you must set fire to the Snee-nee-iq."

The girl opened her mouth to protest, out of habit. But a flash from the big, busy, mouse eyes made her dash into the hut, where she picked up the torch flaming near the door. Then she started down the mountain, slipping, scrambling, slipping, but hanging on to the torch.

The Snee-nee-iq lay like a log at the foot of the steep slope. The girl, shuddering at what she had brought on herself, touched the torch to the giantess.

Like a tree struck by lightning, the Snee-nee-iq burst into flame.

The girl huddled back close to tiny Mouse Woman. But not for long! For, as the Snee-nee-iq was consumed by the fire, ashes rose. And every ash took wing, turning into a small, fierce mosquito. With a horde of angry mosquitoes pursuing her, the girl had no trouble at all getting down the mountain.

She was scratched and bruised and bitten and bitten. But at last she reached the village. She rushed into her own house, and flung herself on her mother. "Why did you let me go?" she stormed. Then, when she had sobbed out her relief at being home again, she whispered, "Never again will I howl for what I want." And she never did.

Yet it was only her family who welcomed her back

to the big cedar house at the foot of the mountain. And nobody at all welcomed the horde of mosquitoes she brought with her.

MOUSE WOMAN did a few merry little hops, skips, and jumps as she bustled back along the Trail-to-the-Place-of-Supernatural-Beings. For somebody *had* done something about the Snee-nee-iq. The small had vanquished the big. And the big had turned into a very small. A girl who had wanted too much had got more than she ever wanted—a horde of mosquitoes. The two who had been upsetting the order of the world had dealt with each other to bring back the order of the world. And it was all very satisfying. Somehow, it made everything equal.

4

Mouse Woman and the Wooden Wife

ONCE IN THE DAYS of very long ago, there was a gifted young chief called Say-oks. He was such a gifted carver that people said the figures on his house posts winked at them. They said the Killer Whale on his canoe spoke to the killer whales in the sea. They said his dance masks opened their eyes and mouths of their own accord, before the dancers pulled the moving-strings. People spoke of his work with awe. For clearly Say-oks had a powerful spirit helper.

Now, he was painting the pattern board for the fringed dancing blanket he would wear on a great occasion. And the eye forms on his pattern board were so lifelike that people said, "That blanket will speak." For in those days, it was well known that life could be woven into a dancing blanket.

But not by Say-oks. For though the painting of the pattern board was man's work, weaving was woman's work.

Fortunately he had just married a chief's daughter

who was a skilled weaver. And when the cottonwoods were golden along the river and a blue haze lay over the mountains, the two of them went off to their mountain camp to hunt goat for the wool they needed for the dancing blanket.

Say-oks, of course, took along his carving tools as well as his hunting gear. And the two of them were very happy in the mountains. While he hunted the goats or carved their horns into beautiful totem-crested spoons, his wife spun the wool into yarn; she dyed some of it black, some green-blue, and some pale yellow for the pattern; and finally she began to weave the dancing blanket.

Then, as winter came to the hills, she took ill and died. The young chief was desolate. For he had loved his wife dearly.

Lost in grief, he tramped through his cold, silent, white world on snowshoes. When the winter stars were glittering in the dark sky and the moon was casting black shadows, he listened to the high song of the wolves and ached with the wild longing of it. When the storms kept him hutbound, he found comfort in his woodworking tools, in carving a figure from red cedar. It was the image of his beautiful young wife. And he carved like one possessed. When the image was finished, it was so lifelike that he set it up before the partly woven blanket, like a woman kneeling. He put his wife's spruce-root hat on its head. He dropped her woolen robe around its shoulders. And using his mask-making skills, he gave it a startling semblance of life. It could turn its head. It could move its fingers.

But it could not weave the blanket.

His wife had woven only the band of black at the top and the narrow strip of blue-green; she had finished only the top of a row of four black eye forms. But already she had woven life into the blanket. And now it sometimes spoke out in the silence. "My eyes will never be finished," it complained, "so I will never see what is happening."

Because he could not bear the loneliness of the camp, the young chief went off every morning with his hunting gear or his axe. And every night he returned. Every night he opened the door of the hut. And that turned his wooden wife's head. Every night he called to it, "Come out, my dear! And see what I have done today."

And every night he answered himself in a woman's

voice. "Oh, I can't come out, my dear. The yarn is twisted around my fingers."

Which, of course, it was. The yarn was twisted around the wooden fingers.

As the days went by, hunters passed the camp and glanced in. And strange rumors began circling the mountains. Strange rumors reached the village.

"A wooden wife!" people gasped. "Yet . . . yet Say-oks has a powerful spirit helper. So . . . perhaps . . . perhaps his wooden wife will come to life." Then they added in awed whispers, "Perhaps the spirit self of his real wife will enter into the cedar." And they stayed carefully away from the awesome mountain camp.

Now there was one tiny person who heard the rumors and did not stay away. This, of course, was Mouse Woman.

"A wooden wife!" she squeaked to herself. And her nose twitched. For this was not a proper thing. So, being the busiest of all busybodies, she bustled along the trail to see about it. When she reached the hunting camp, she went into the hut. And though her ravelly little fingers itched, she did not touch the wool she saw piled up around the wooden figure. For that would not have been proper.

Then she heard something.

"My eyes will never be finished," she heard the dancing blanket complain, "so I will never see what is happening."

Mouse Woman's nose twitched. For this, too, was not a proper thing. Anything that was started should be finished—especially a dancing blanket!

Late in the day she heard the young chief return-
ing. So she transformed herself into a white mouse
and watched and listened from behind a pile of wool.

The door opened. The wooden wife's head turned.

"Come out, my dear!" the young man called. "And
see what I have done today."

"Oh, I can't come out, my dear," he answered himself in a woman's voice. "The yarn is twisted around
my fingers."

Peering out through the pile of wool, Mouse
Woman watched and listened. And as soon as he
had gone off to fetch firewood, she spirited herself
back along the trail.

"Well!" she squeaked to herself when she reached
home. And now her nose really twitched. For a
wooden wife was not a proper thing for a handsome
young chief. If mischief-makers heard about it, who
knew where it would all end?

"No man should have a knothead wife!" she told
herself indignantly. "No man should be married to a
spouse of splinters! Someone must do something!"

Alert for the someone who could do the something
about it, she really began to watch the world with
her big, busy, mouse eyes.

Now IT HAPPENED that a great chief's daughter from a
faraway village was roaming about in those mountains. She had been captured, and had escaped after a
long, hard journey. She was cold and hungry. She
was weary of snowshoes, weary of snow shelters,
weary of setting out snares to get something to eat.

"She is the someone," Mouse Woman told herself. And being the busiest of busybodies, she

planned to make the young woman do the something. First, she spirited her house to the side of a likely trail. Then, as soon as she glimpsed the princess stumbling along the trail on snowshoes, the narnauk transformed herself into a white mouse. A lame white mouse. For, of course, the princess must be tested. Mouse Woman was a stickler for worthy behavior.

By and by the princess came along, weary and cold and hungry. Her fur robe was in tatters, her dark hair in tangles. Trudging along with a drooping head, she saw the lame mouse trying to climb over a big log. Being lame, it kept falling off.

"Poor little mouse!" said the princess, trudging over to help it. She lifted it gently over the log. And she watched it with compassionate eyes as it disappeared into a grove of alpine fir trees.

Then she heard a voice call from the grove. "Come in, my dear!" it commanded in an imperious little squeak.

Surprised by the command, as well as by the squeaky little voice in which it was given, the girl went timidly into the grove. And there, to her amazement, was a house decorated all over with Mouse totems.

"Come in, my dear!" the imperious squeak commanded.

So she went in. And there was the tiniest grandmother she had ever seen.

"Mouse Woman!" she cried out. And her shoulders sagged with relief. For it was well known that Mouse Woman was a friend to young people in distress. "Mouse Woman!" she said again, in an awed whisper. For Mouse Woman was also a narnauk.

"Sit down, my dear!" Mouse Woman invited, as imperiously as if she had been tree-tall. "You have been kind to me, so I will repay your kindness." She took one longing look at the girl's long woolen ear tassels before she bustled off to fetch a steaming bowl of meat.

The princess sank down onto a mat beside the fire. And she gratefully took the food Mouse Woman offered.

Mouse Woman stood watching with her big, busy, mouse eyes. And though her ravelly little fingers itched, she did not poke the long woolen ear tassels to set them swinging. "Can you weave?" she asked the princess.

The girl nodded. For she was a skilled weaver.

Mouse Woman beamed. The girl was a skilled weaver. She was kind. And by her ornaments, she was clearly a Wolf princess, like the young chief's dead wife. She was indeed the someone. Mouse Woman was so pleased that she allowed herself to reach out and set one tassel swinging. "Now, my dear, you must have a good sleep," she said kindly. "We will talk of things in the morning."

When morning came, the imperious little narnauk said, "Now, my dear, when you have eaten, you must follow a certain trail. And you will see what you will see; you will do what you will do." She did not say what the princess would see or what she would do. She merely gave her careful directions to the place where she would go.

THE GIRL FOLLOWED the certain trail, and at last she reached Say-oks's hunting camp. But still fearful of anyone in these strange mountains, she hid herself to watch and listen.

By and by, she saw the young chief come home. He was a very handsome young chief. She saw him open the door of the hut. She heard him call, "Come out, my dear! And see what I have done today."

Then she heard a very strange thing. "Oh, I can't come out, my dear," he answered himself in a woman's voice. "The yarn is twisted around my fingers."

The girl was so curious about what had happened that, as soon as he had gone off to fetch firewood, she crept to the door of the hut and glanced in. She saw the figure kneeling in front of the partly woven blanket.

"The wooden wife!" she gasped. For she had heard the story one day while she was keeping herself hidden from two passing hunters. This was the young man who had lost his wife. "The poor man!" she murmured. And compassion flooded through her. But fearful of intruding on his grief, she again hid herself.

That night she heard the high, wild singing of the wolves and shivered in her snow shelter. By morning she was very cold and very, very hungry. So, as soon as Say-oks had gone off with his hunting gear, she crept into the hut to warm herself. And there she saw a strange thing. There was hot meat steaming in a bowl by the wooden figure. "Oh, the poor man!" she murmured. For clearly he was pretending that the wooden wife could eat as well as speak.

She looked at the meat with longing eyes. She sniffed the delicious aroma. For she was very, very hungry.

Suddenly, she jumped at the sound of a voice.

"My eyes will never be finished," the voice complained, "so I will never see what is happening."

"The blanket!" she gasped. Clearly it had already taken on life. But it would never be finished. It would always be like a person with part of a head and no body.

"Poor blanket!" she murmured. And her weaver's fingers itched to complete the lovely design she saw on the pattern board.

She glanced at the meat again. She glanced at the pattern board. "Perhaps . . ." she murmured. Perhaps she could eat a bit of the meat and repay the young chief with a bit of weaving. For clearly he cared about the dancing blanket.

So she ate a bit of the meat. She wove a bit of the blanket. Then she carefully twisted the yarn once more around the wooden fingers. And once more hiding herself, she waited to see what she would see, as Mouse Woman had suggested.

By and by the young chief came home. He opened the hut door and called, "Come out, my dear! And see what I have done today."

"Oh, I can't come out, my dear," he answered himself in a woman's voice. "The yarn is twisted around my fingers."

"The poor man!" the watching princess murmured. Filled with compassion for the young man's longing for his wife, she watched him go into the hut. And she pressed her ear to a crack to hear what would happen.

"My dear!" he cried out in amazement. "You have

. . . eaten . . . some of the meat? It can't be. Yet
. . ." Then he cried out again in amazement. "My
dear! You have done a little weaving? It can't be.
Yet . . ." Now his voice rang with hope as well as
amazement.

The listening princess swallowed. The poor young
man thought his wooden wife was indeed taking on
life. "What have I done?" she whispered. "And what
must I do now?"

She decided to wait for morning.

That night, again, she heard the high, wild singing
of the wolves and shivered in her snow shelter. By
morning, she was so cold and so hungry that, as soon
as Say-oks had gone off with his axe, she again crept
into the hut to warm herself. Again she was tempted
by the steaming hot meat and its delicious aroma.
Again the blanket cried out. "My eyes will never be
finished," it complained, "so I will never see what is
happening."

"Poor blanket!" she murmured. And again her
weaver's fingers itched to complete the lovely pattern.

So, again she ate some of the meat. Again she did
a bit of weaving. Again she twisted the yarn around
the wooden fingers. Again she hid herself before
Say-oks came home. And again she was filled with
compassion as he opened the door of the hut and
called, "Come out, my dear! And see what I have
done today."

Again he answered himself in a woman's voice.
"Oh, I can't come out, my dear. The yarn is twisted
around my fingers." And this time he darted eagerly

into the hut to see what had happened to the meat and to the blanket.

Listening again through the crack, the princess heard him cry out, "My dear! You have eaten . . . more of the meat? It can't be. Yet . . ." Then again he cried out, "My dear! You have done more of the weaving? It can't be. Yet . . ." And now his voice really rang with hope as well as amazement.

"The poor man!" the listening girl murmured. "What have I done? And what must I do now?"

Again she decided to wait for morning.

And again the same things happened.

By the fourth morning, she knew what she must do. As soon as Say-oks had gone off with his hunting gear, she darted into the hut. She ate the steaming meat. Then she untwisted the yarn from the wooden fingers. She took the spruce-root hat off the wooden head. She took the woolen robe off the wooden shoulders. She dragged the light cedar image out behind the hut. And, thankful that dry cedar burned quickly, she burned the wooden wife.

Then, with a thudding heart, she put the spruce-root hat on her own head. She put the woolen robe on her own shoulders. She knelt before the blanket and started weaving. And for the rest of the day she wove and wove the dancing blanket.

Terror seized her when she heard Say-oks come home.

He opened the door of the hut.

She turned her head as the wooden wife had turned its head.

"Come out, my dear!" he called. "And see what I have done today."

Before he could answer himself in a woman's voice, she managed to cry out, "Oh, I can't come out, my dear. The yarn is twisted around my fingers."

The stunned man stood still. Then he darted toward the figure kneeling in front of the dancing blanket. "My dear!" he cried out in pure joy. "You have eaten all the meat. And you have finished weaving the eyes. It can't be. Yet . . ."

Yet it was. Clearly the wooden wife had come to life. Clearly the spirit self of his dead wife had entered into the cedar. He pulled the princess to her feet and warmly embraced her. And the two were very happy in the hut in the mountains.

As the days passed, the sun warmed the mountain valley. Land otters tobogganed merrily down a slope into a lake near the hunting camp. Wolves filled the nights with their singing, while the Northern Lights crackled and painted the snow peaks with rainbow tints. And the two were very, very happy.

One day two hunters chanced to pass the hut and glance in. They saw the figure kneeling before the dancing blanket. They heard her singing. So they rushed home to tell the village.

"The wooden wife!" people gasped. "It *has* taken on life?" That couldn't be. "Yet, Say-oks has a powerful spirit helper," they reminded one another. And they began to watch the trail for the coming of the young couple.

Say-oks and his wife came with the springtime. Birds were warbling in the budding trees. Violet-green swallows swooped and darted along the river bank. Great white swans passed high overhead, trumpeting a greeting. But the people greeted Say-oks and his wife with quiet awe. For this was a very, very strange thing that had happened.

"She looks different now," women whispered to one another. Clearly Say-oks had not carved a perfect image of his dead wife. Also, she was strangely vague about who people were. But then, she had been dead for a time, they reminded one another. At least her weaving was as skillful as it had always been. They watched the dancing blanket grow, day by day, into a lovely, fringed, patterned mantle.

When it was finally finished, she began to weave another, a very tiny dancing blanket.

"Why?" people asked one another. For such a mantle could be worn only by chiefs. And what chief was that small?

"Why?" they asked one another again.

But nobody could think why. And Say-oks's wife told them nothing.

Then, once more it was winter. People were gathered in the feasthouse for a great occasion. Wearing colorful regalia, they were feasting and settling the affairs of the people. They were drumming and chanting and dancing and telling stories.

The young chief put on his new dancing blanket and a chief's headdress ringed with sea otter bristles. And while drums thudded through the great cedar house and people chanted, Say-oks did his chief's dance around the fire. As he danced, his beautiful new dancing blanket swirled its graceful fringes.

Then a very strange thing happened. A white mouse appeared. It vanished. And there in its place stood the tiniest grandmother anyone had ever seen.

She was wearing the tiny dancing blanket.

"Mouse Woman!" people cried out. Then they hushed themselves with awe. For Mouse Woman was a narnauk. As well as a Chief-woman. But why was she here? And why was she wearing the wooden wife's dancing blanket?

Nobody could think why. But as Mouse Woman did a merry little mouse dance around the fire, people said that the figures on Say-oks's house posts winked at her. They said that his new dancing blanket spoke to her.

And perhaps the blanket did speak. Perhaps it spoke to other people, too. For, if it did not speak, who ever told the people what had really happened up in the mountains?

Certainly not Mouse Woman, who vanished after her merry little mouse dance. She did a few little hops, skips, and jumps as she bustled back along her trail. For things were strangely satisfying. Someone had done something. What had been started had been finished. Say-oks had a proper wife instead of a knothead, instead of a spouse of splinters. And the dancing blanket now had so many eyes that it could see what was happening all around it.

After finding pleasure so often in the woolen things her ravelly little fingers tore into a lovely, loose, nesty pile of wool, Mouse Woman was glad to have given pleasure to a woolen thing. Somehow, it made everything equal.

5

Mouse Woman and the Monster Killer Whale

IT WAS IN THE TIME of long ago, when things were very, very different. Then, supernatural beings roamed the vast wildernesses of the Northwest Coast. And Mouse Woman kept a close watch on what these narnauks did to the Real People.

At that time, the Real People were often out on the sea in their great totem-crested canoes. For they were sea hunters as well as fishermen and land hunters; they were families who moved from place to place by water. And because the sea was deep and cold, because there were wild storms and fogs and rip tides, the Real People moved in awe of the Ocean People who could help them or harm them. People were careful never to spit into the sea. They were careful to offer gifts to the Great Killer Whale and the Great Sea Lion and the Great Sea Otter and other spirit beings. And they were even more careful not to offend the Sea Monsters. Their fear of Great-Whirlpool-Maker and the Giant Devilfish and the Five-

Finned-Whale and the Monster Killer Whale kept them wafting eagle down—the symbol of peace and friendship—on certain waters.

And it kept Mouse Woman watching the sea with her big, busy, mouse eyes, even though the sea was none of her business.

At the moment, it was the Monster Killer Whale who had her nose twitching. *He* had taken to snatching beautiful young women away from their proper husbands.

"It's time somebody did something about that monster," she told herself, without a thought for *his* size and *her* size, or a thought for the sea being none of her business.

Now at that time the lustrous black pelts of the sea otter were in great demand for chief's robes. And one young sea hunter of the Wolf Crest, Na-na-simgat, was so successful in catching them that he may have angered the Great Sea Otter. And *he* may have helped the Monster Killer Whale to capture Na-na-simgat's beautiful young wife.

Whatever the reason, a very strange thing happened.

One day a white sea otter came into the bay in front of Na-na-simgat's village. And for several days it swam about close to the shore.

"A white sea otter?" people murmured, with some awe. For no one had ever before seen a white sea otter.

Finally, Na-na-simgat could not resist the challenge. He went out on the bay and shot the white sea otter. And though he was careful to send his arrow through the tail, not to harm the rare pelt, though his men were careful in taking it ashore and even more careful in skinning it, there were blood stains on the white fur.

"Such beautiful fur!" his wife said, stroking the lustrous white pelt. "I shall stay here and cleanse it in the sea."

So it was that while the others went back to their houses, she stayed alone at the edge of the sea, washing the white fur in the splashing surf. Concerned for the strangely strong tug of the sea, she stood on one edge of the fur, to anchor it.

Yet the sea tugged it from her.

"Oh!" she gasped. "I can't lose this beautiful skin." So she waded out into the water and grabbed it.

But again the tug of the sea caught it. And this time it pulled the fur out into deep water.

"Oh!" she gasped. "I can't lose this beautiful skin." So she swam out after it. And just as she was reaching for it, a killer whale surfaced right under her and carried her off.

Terrified, she clung to the whale's dorsal fin while the great black and white beast raced away through the waters.

After some time, when she did not return to the house, Na-na-simgat was anxious about her. He ran down to the beach. But his wife was gone.

What could have happened to her?

He raised the alarm in the village, and people searched the shoreline. They went out on the water. But there was no trace of her, anywhere. And no

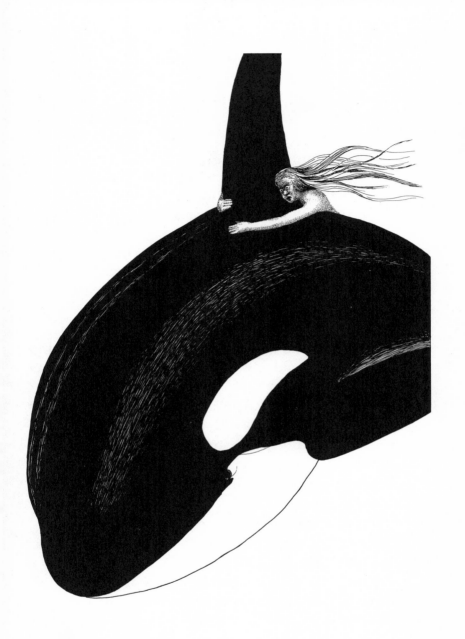

trace of the white sea otter pelt.

Na-na-simgat was desolate. For he loved his wife dearly.

What could have happened to her?

Clearly there was only one way to find out. So he called the famous shaman.

The shaman put on a dancing apron that clattered with bird beaks. He put a crown of grizzly bear claws over his long straggly grey hair. He picked up his medicine rattle and his white eagle tail feather. Then, as clappers clacked and plank drums thudded hypnotically through the big windowless house, he began to circle the fire in a wild leaping dance. The dance grew wilder and faster, wilder and faster, wilder and faster, until suddenly the shaman collapsed and lay as though dead.

The people hushed themselves. For the shaman's spirit self had left its body to make a spirit journey in search of the lost wife.

At long, long last he seemed to stir. So the people began to chant softly, luring his spirit self back to its body.

Then he sat up. And his eyes were a wild glitter.

"She has been carried off to the Mountain of Qwawk," he said.

People gasped in horror. For the Mountain of Qwawk was in the spirit world under the ocean. It was the home of the Monster Killer Whale. And it was guarded by a fearsome double-headed monster. The people almost held their breath to hear what else the shaman would tell them.

"The gateway to the Mountain of Qwawk is

marked by two great kelp heads," he went on. And his eyes were still a wild glitter. "But they can be found only with the help of spirit beings. And they can be reached only by a certain canoe that will be found on the shore at the end of a journey."

People gasped. For it would be a fearsome journey, into the spirit world. All eyes turned on Na-na-simgat.

"I have the Marten and the Swallow," he reminded them boldly. They were his two guardian spirits, invisible to other people, but visible to him. "They will help me, first, to find the canoe, and then to find the two great kelp heads that mark the gateway to the Mountain of Qwawk."

To strengthen his own spirit power for the journey, he fasted and prayed. Then he chewed devil's club and cleansed himself with sea water. He put many pieces of mountain goat fat into a large pouch; for it was well known that the Ocean People always craved fat. And into a smaller pouch he put the sacred herbs that his spirit guardians had given him. He would need much spirit aid on so perilous a journey.

When all was ready, he started out.

His glossy little Marten went ahead of him, sniffing the earth and the air for what his nose could tell him; while his graceful Swallow wheeled and darted above him, riding the invisible air waves as he sought the way to the only canoe that could reach the two great kelp heads that marked the gateway into the Mountain of Qwawk. The lovely bird brightened the world for Na-na-simgat with flashes of green and violet, and the shining whiteness of its underbody.

They travelled for a long, long time. Sometimes Na-na-simgat grew weary. But always his longing for his beautiful young wife urged him on and on. Always his glossy little Marten went ahead, sniffing the earth and the air for what his nose could tell him. And always his graceful Swallow wheeled and darted above him, seeking the way to the only canoe that could reach the two great kelp heads that marked the gateway into the Mountain of Qwawk.

Then one day he sensed excitement in the sniffing and wriggling of his glossy little Marten. He saw joy in the swoops and sweeps of his graceful Swallow.

They had found the canoe.

It was a strange canoe, carved and painted so powerfully in sea patterns that its seaweeds seemed to wash and wave; its starfish seemed to move among them.

"It's only the reflections of the moving water," Na-na-simgat told himself. But he stepped into the canoe with awed respect for its spirit power. His glossy little Marten bounded onto the high prow to sniff the ocean breezes. And his graceful Swallow wheeled and darted above them, riding the invisible air waves.

Na-na-simgat grasped the paddle. But the strange canoe seemed to move almost of itself, following the flight of the Swallow. It moved off from the shore, out through the narrow channel, out past the green fringe of islands, out beyond the reefs where the surf was as white as the flashing sea gulls. It moved out into the vast lonely spaces of the ocean. On and on and on and on it went.

Then once more Na-na-simgat sensed excitement in the sniffing and wriggling of his glossy little Marten. He saw joy in the swoops and sweeps of his graceful Swallow.

They had found the kelp heads.

They were strange kelp heads; dark as a wet seal's body; wide as an eagle's wingspan; rising and falling in the mighty sea swells, in the quiet of the lonely ocean. And nearby was a floating platform of tangled kelp tubes: dark as a herd of wet seals; wide as the wingspan of many eagles; rising and falling, washing and weaving in the mighty sea swells, in the quiet of the lonely ocean.

"PHWUUUUUUUUUUUUUU!"

The terrifying sound made Na-na-simgat jump. "PHWUUUUUUUUUUUUUU!" Like the screaming whistle of a thousand killer whales shrieking through their blow holes.

"The blow hole of the Mountain of Qwawk!" he murmured as he saw the dark peak of the mountain under the water. Swallowing his terror, he peered down below the two great kelp heads, and he caught his breath. For there was a ladder. The two great kelp heads were the top of a kelp ladder, a ladder that moved with the movement of the ocean.

That was the way into the Mountain of Qwawk; the way to the house of the Monster Killer Whale. And somewhere that house was guarded by a fearsome double-headed monster. The sea hunter's shoulders sagged in despair.

Then they lifted and squared with purpose. That ladder was the way to his beautiful lost wife.

"Wait here for me," he said to his guardian spirits. For they could go no farther with him.

He tied the canoe to the floating platform of tangled kelp tubes, and he dived into the sea and swam toward the fearsome ladder. Before he reached it, though, he treaded water while he filled his lungs with sea air. Then he reached for the ladder.

But just as he was reaching for it, a killer whale surfaced right under him and carried him off.

Terrified, he clung to its dorsal fin as the great black and white beast circled through the waters. Then, expecting a dive, he took another gulp of sea air.

The killer whale dived. And Na-na-simgat, still clinging to the dorsal fin, felt the rush of the water. Almost before he could blink his eyes, he was flung off, through an opened doorway. And the door closed behind him fast, like the shut of a clam shell.

He was alone in a strange world. Alone in the spirit world of the Ocean People, under the ocean.

There were trees, but not trees as he knew them. For they seemed almost to wash and wave, as though an invisible sea moved through them. And there was a marsh at his feet, a marsh with reeds that also seemed to wave and wash as though an invisible sea moved through them. It was strange and terrifying.

But there was no sign of the fearsome double-headed monster. Perhaps he was watching from beyond the waving trees. Na-na-simgat swallowed.

Then he saw something moving in the reeds.

"Geese!" He scarcely breathed it.

But they were not geese as he knew them. These

geese were grubbing among the reeds, bumping into one another and hissing angrily as they bumped.

Peering closer, he saw that they were blind. Their eyelids were closed, as if by some spell.

With instant compassion, he opened his small pouch, took out a few leaves of his sacred herbs, chewed them, spat on his hands, and murmuring softly to one goose, he touched her eyelids with his fingers.

Her eyes opened.

"I can see!" she cried out, speaking like a Real Person. Then she hushed herself and glanced fearfully about, as if fearing that somebody heard her.

"I can see!" she said again, in a grateful whisper.

So, murmuring softly to all the geese in turn, Na-na-simgat touched their eyelids. And all their eyes opened.

"I can see!" each cried out, speaking like a Real Person. Then each hushed herself and glanced fearfully about, as if fearing that somebody heard her.

At last all could see and speak.

"Once we were women," the first goose whispered to Na-na-simgat, "carried off to be the wives of the Monster Killer Whale. But as soon as we were no longer young and beautiful, we were made slaves. Then changed into geese, blind geese who would be startled by any stranger who came along and so give the alarm to our master's guard." Again she glanced fearfully about, as if fearing that somebody heard her.

Then she stiffened. All the geese stiffened. They stretched out their necks and hissed toward the place where a path led through a narrow cut in the rocks.

"Dzenk!" the first goose warned Na-na-simgat, while she and the other geese went back to grubbing among the weeds. Sometimes they bumped into one another and hissed angrily as they bumped, acting as if they were still blind, as if nothing had happened.

Na-na-simgat hid himself behind a clump of ferns that waved as the trees and the reeds waved, as if an invisible sea were washing through them. And he almost held his breath when he peered out through the tall fronds.

Soon he saw Dzenk emerging from the cut in the rocks. Dzenk! The Monster Killer Whale's guard. He was a fearsome being, like a man, yet strangely like a fish, too. He had two heads. And the heads kept looking around in different directions, the fishy eyes peering this way and that way.

Na-na-simgat shivered. For it was well known that Dzenk had a terrible power. If he grew angry, he could swell up to block any passage. Nobody could get past him.

SQUEAK!

Na-na-simgat jumped at a sudden sound behind him.

"Have you any fat?" a voice said, so suddenly that he jumped again. It was a small, squeaky voice that seemed to come from down low behind him. Yet when he glanced back, there was nobody near him.

"Have you any fat?" the voice asked again. And though it was still small and squeaky, he knew it for the voice of a Chief-woman.

He glanced back again. And there was Mouse

Woman, watching him with her big, busy, mouse eyes. "Have you any fat?" she demanded. And now her nose twitched.

"Yes, Grandmother," Na-na-simgat answered, as soon as he was over his surprise. And he indicated the large pouch that was crammed with pieces of mountain goat fat.

"Give it to me, my dear!" Mouse Woman ordered. "For I can make better use of it than you can."

"Yes, Grandmother," he agreed. He gave her the pouch, though it seemed a heavy pouch for such a tiny narnauk. But as he did, he glanced fearfully toward the spot where Dzenk was now sitting against a tree, waving with the tree's waving.

"Leave him to me, my dear!" Mouse Woman ordered. And she bustled off to speak to the fearsome monster who was like a man, yet strangely like a fish, too. His two heads were still looking around in different directions. Until one of them saw Mouse Woman.

"YOU!" that head thundered; while both faces scowled at the busiest of busy bodies. The sea, after all, was none of her business.

"Fortunately for you, yes," she answered, taking a piece of mountain goat fat out of the large pouch.

The monster's four fishy eyes looked greedily at the fat. His two tongues licked his four lips as the tiny narnauk began rolling the fat in her hands in a very peculiar manner. When she held it out to him, he snatched it and put it into one mouth . . . then the other mouth . . . then the first again, as if neither mouth could bear to be without it.

Then Na-na-simgat, peering through the fern fronds, saw a very strange thing happen. The transfer of the fat from one mouth to the other grew slower and slower. The fishy eyes glazed with sleep. The two heads began to nod. And the monster began to snore, with a snore that was like thunder.

Na-na-simgat shivered, listening to it from behind the fern fronds.

But Mouse Woman soon stopped his shivering. "Now be on your way!" she ordered. She pointed to the path that led through the narrow cut in the rocks. "And find what you came for!" She gave him back the large pouch.

Na-na-simgat went on his way, alert for what he might find beyond the narrow cut in the rocks. And soon he found himself following a path through a forest of trees that waved as the other trees had waved, as if an invisible sea were washing through them.

He had not gone far into the forest before he came, suddenly, to three small men who were cutting down an old hollow hemlock tree.

At sight of a stranger, they dropped their axe and huddled together.

"We're just getting wood," one of them said.

"For our master," another added quickly.

"And it must be dry hemlock or he'll punish us," the third said.

They were the strangest looking men! The color of a red cod. They had huge heads tapering down into narrow bodies without benefit of a neck or shoulders. Their lower jaws jutted ahead of their wide mouths,

and their bulbous eyes bulged in their ugly flat faces.

"Go on with your work," Na-na-simgat said kindly. And the three tripped over roots in their rush to get the dry hemlock for their terrifying master. The one with the axe hit the hollow tree with such energy that his axe broke.

Now the three really huddled together.

"Our master will punish us," all three of them blubbered.

"Not if I can mend the axe," Na-na-simgat said kindly.

All three stopped blubbering. All three opened and closed their wide mouths as they tried to think of what they might say.

"Your master is the Monster Killer Whale?" Na-na-simgat asked as he took a pinch of sacred herbs out of his small pouch.

All three nodded their red bodies, while their wide mouths still worked to say something.

"And he has captured a beautiful young human for a wife?" Na-na-simgat asked as he started to chew the herbs.

All three nodded their red bodies, while their wide mouths still worked to say something.

"And you will help me if I help you?" Na-na-simgat bargained when he had spat on his hands.

All three nodded their red bodies while their wide mouths managed to cry out, "Yes! Yes! Yes!" And now that they had finally found their voices, they jabbered together.

"He's going to turn her—"

"Into what he is."

"So she won't grow old and—"

"Have to be turned into a goose."

"A blind goose."

Hearing them as he rubbed his hands over the broken axe, Na-na-simgat's eyes flashed. His mouth clamped shut.

Then the parts of the axe came together. As good as new.

Grabbing it thankfully, the three slaves stumbled over roots in their rush to get the dry hemlock for their terrifying master. Not until it was ready did they listen to the plan for the rescue of the beautiful young wife. And as they listened, they nodded their red bodies in agreement while their wide mouths worked to impress the plan on their minds.

"I will take the water to the fire," the first slave said, to be sure he had the plan straight.

"I will put my wood down close to his water," the second slave said.

"And I will start to throw my wood on the fire," the third said. "Only I will trip over *his* wood and knock over *his* water."

"Which will make a great fog," Na-na-simgat went on, "so I can snatch up my wife." His voice was strong. But his eyes were anxious. For he did wish he had a good way to get into the house. He did wish he had a good way to warn his wife not to seem to recognize him or else not to cry out and resist when somebody grabbed her whom she did not recognize as her husband. Most of all, he did wish he had a way to put the Monster Killer Whale to sleep as Mouse Woman had put the guard to sleep—even if the snoring might deafen him.

The third slave's eyes were as anxious as Na-na-simgat's. "I do hope I can trip," he said.

"Oh, you'll trip," the sea hunter assured him. He only wished everything else was as sure as the slave's tripping. For all three slaves were masters at tripping.

"But now, what'll they do with the killer whale robe?" the second slave wondered.

"And with the dorsal fin they're making?" the third added.

"What robe? What dorsal fin?" Na-na-simgat asked them.

The slaves told him about it as they all followed the path to the Monster Killer Whale's house.

"They're making a killer whale robe for your wife."

"And a dorsal fin."

"So they can turn her into a killer whale before the Monster takes her for his wife."

Before Na-na-simgat could say that this would never happen, another voice spoke up, a small, squeaky voice that seemed to come from down low, behind him. "Wait!" the voice said.

"Mouse Woman!" he cried out, thankful that she had turned up again. He spun round. And there she was, looking up at him with her big, busy, mouse eyes.

"Hide behind the house, my dear!" she ordered, in the voice of a Chief-woman. And her nose twitched.

"Yes, Grandmother," Na-na-simgat answered. As he neared the house, he crept around to the back and watched through a big crack. Mouse Woman had taken over!

Then he caught his breath. For he saw his wife, warming herself by the fire. She looked very forlorn there in the vast murky house of the Killer Whale Monster. But, even as he watched, a mouse scurried up onto her shoulder. He saw his wife start. Then he saw her stand very quietly, alert for what was to happen.

Mouse Woman had taken over.

Mouse Woman had indeed taken over. Suddenly, there she was, confronting the Monster who sat at the rear of the fire. He was like a giant man, yet like a whale, too, with his small eyes and his enormous mouth set with conical teeth.

"YOU!" he thundered, glaring at the tiny narnauk.

"Fortunately for you, yes," she answered. "For there is fat in this for you."

"FAT!" The Monster sat up. And his huge mouth slavered. "Where is the fat?" he thundered at her.

"A grandson has it," she answered calmly. She did not say *whose* grandson. "And he wishes to feast you."

"A GRANDSON?" the Monster roared, clearly angry that anyone had managed to get past the guard, Dzenk. Then his mouth slavered again. "Tell him to bring the fat in!" he ordered.

Mouse Woman bustled toward the door. The watching sea hunter slipped around the house to meet her; while the three slaves just stood there with their wood and water, waiting for their part in the rescue of the beautiful young wife.

Mouse Woman whispered to the three small men who were so strangely like red cod. Then she turned to Na-na-simgat. "When the time comes, give the fat to me, my dear!" she ordered. "For I can make better use of it than you can." Her tiny nose twitched.

"Yes, Grandmother," he agreed gratefully. And he followed her into the vast murkiness of the Monster Killer Whale's house. He kept his eyes carefully away from his wife as he followed the tiny narnauk to the rear of the fire.

"Sit down, Grandson!" the Monster Killer Whale invited. His mouth slavered as he watched the young man take the large pouch from his waist and hand it to Mouse Woman.

She opened the pouch, rolled the pieces of fat in a very peculiar manner, put the fat in the fire, spirited it out again, and . . . and a very strange thing happened. Where there had been a small pile of mountain goat fat, now there was an enormous pile. All around the fire, wide, fishy mouths were slavering.

Soon the Monster Killer Whale and his relatives were greedily chewing the fat. As they chewed it, the chewing grew slower and slower; the fishy eyes glazed with sleep; heads began to nod, lower and lower.

The young man held his breath.

Then—before the monsters were really asleep and snoring!—the three slaves stumbled and bumbled in with their wood and water, terrified of the Monster Killer Whale, terrified of his relatives, terrified of not doing their part right.

Now Na-na-simgat really held his breath.

The first put his water near the fire.

The second put his wood near the water.

And the third, lurching to throw his wood on the

fire, actually did trip over the other wood and knock over the water.

There was a great hiss. A murky fog filled the air around the fire.

Na-na-simgat leaped up. He snatched up his wife's hand. And the two of them raced for the door.

But the Monster and his relatives were not quite asleep yet. Jerked upright by the commotion, they staggered to their feet with screaming whistles, like a score of killer whales shrieking through their blow holes. They bumped and jostled and staggered after the young couple. Their commotion gave the alarm to other relatives who were doing things outside.

These relatives took out after Na-na-simgat and the beautiful young wife he was stealing away from their own beloved Monster.

The couple had a good head start. But as the chase swept along the path like a gale through the forest, the relatives began to close the gap.

The chase swept on and on. Then Na-na-simgat saw the narrow cut in the rocks. And his heart fell. For he saw Dzenk, too.

And Dzenk saw them. Rudely roused from his sleep by the commotion, the Monster's guard staggered into the narrow cut in the rocks. Charged by his own anger, he began to swell up.

He would block their passage. Na-na-simgat groaned.

But a gaggle of geese, no longer blind, hissed at the Monster's guard. They flew at him. They pecked at him from all sides and from all heights. And the flailing guard, looking this way and that way to fight off the attack, knocked his two heads together with such a crack that he fell down.

While the avenging geese kept the monster busy, Na-na-simgat and his wife clambered over him and around him. Then wild with anger, Dzenk regained his feet. But now his own anger defeated him. For he swelled up so big that he stuck fast in the narrow cut. And the thundering relatives could not budge him to go after the escaping couple.

They were at the doorway of the Mountain of Qwawk.

But how could they open it?

They both sagged in despair.

How could they get out?

"Leave it to me, my dears," a squeaky little voice said. The most wonderful, welcome, thrilling, squeaky little voice they had ever heard.

"Yes, Grandmother," they both gasped in relief.

The tiny narnauk touched something. The door opened for an instant—the instant they needed. Then it closed behind them, fast, like the shut of a clam shell. And they were out in the sea, at the foot of the kelp ladder.

They saw the ladder, but they saw something else, too. Killer whales! Coming at them from all directions, with their mouths open.

At that desperate moment, a wonderful thing happened. Shoals of red cod shot into the space between the killer whales and the young man who had been helpful to three captured Red Cod People, who had been turned into slaves by the Monster Killer Whale. In a great darting, glinting red mass, in a beautiful ripple of fins, they WHOOSHED the young couple upward, sending them on their way to the surface.

Na-na-simgat saw the undersurface of the sea. It was like a shining blue-green spirit blanket waving and rippling in the light of the Real World.

They broke surface. And there was the canoe tied to the floating platform of tangled kelp tubes. There were Na-na-simgat's spirit helpers.

Only he saw the glossy little Marten wriggle with delight, while the graceful Swallow wheeled and darted and swooped for joy. For his spirit helpers were invisible to other people. But they were visible to him as they guided him and his beautiful young wife back to their own village.

When they were safely home, drums thudded in the great feasthouse in the village. Voices chanted. Dancers whirled and leaped around the fire in their fringed dancing blankets.

Then, suddenly, Mouse Woman stood there, watching it all with her big, busy, mouse eyes. And people hushed themselves in awe. For Mouse Woman was a narnauk.

Na-na-simgat's wife cried out, "Mouse Woman!" She threw her long woolen ear tassels into the fire. And before they were more than scorched, Mouse Woman spirited them out. Her ravelly little fingers began tearing them into a lovely, loose, nesty pile of mountain sheep wool. Clearly it was very satisfying.

It was very, very satisfying to Mouse Woman. For somebody had done something about that Monster

Killer Whale. A helpful one had been helped; a small had vanquished a big, making all things equal. And a human wife had been restored to her human husband, bringing order back to the world.

Then Mouse Woman vanished.

6

Mouse Woman and the Daughter of the Sun

ONCE THERE WAS a village whose totem pole houses and totem-crested canoes edged a lonely little beach on the Northwest Coast. The village was bright with the carved and painted emblems of the people: Eagle, Raven, Bear, Wolf, Frog, Killer Whale . . .

Yet often it was dark, too, with the darkness of the rain coast. Especially in winter, storms darkened the sea and rain shrouded the dark green forest that rose up the mountain behind the village. And people wore shredded cedar bark robes and rain hats woven from spruce roots. The hats were beautifully painted with the emblems of their owners.

Now there was in those days someone who longed to come to the rain coast to see how it was in the beautiful little village when storm clouds hid it from a Sky view. This someone was a daughter of the Sun. She lived in the dazzling brightness of the Sun's house, and for centuries she had longed to come down and see how it was.

91

At that time in this village there was a youth known as Sun Cloud; for though his face was as dull as a rain cloud hiding the sun, everyone knew that his warmth and brightness were always there behind the face. And people loved him.

In the same village there was a girl who was known as Snow Flower. Though *her* face was as beautiful as an early mountain flower, her coldness was as forbidding as the snowbank behind which it bloomed. Nobody loved Snow Flower.

Nobody except Sun Cloud.

Since they were cousins, Sun Cloud and Snow Flower had grown up in each other's company. As children they had fished together and gathered berries together; they had gone out on the sea together. And Sun Cloud had always been so sunny and kind to his cousin that he had never even noticed *her* coldness, *her* unkindness. All he had noticed was her beauty, which seemed to blossom in the warmth of his attention. And as the years passed and Snow Flower grew even lovelier, Sun Cloud wanted to be always in the presence of such beauty. So he asked her to marry him.

Since the two young people were of properly similar high rank and of properly different crests, the match was approved by everyone.

Everyone, except Snow Flower.

Vain of her own beauty, Snow Flower craved the attention she received on all sides. Every youth wanted to be seen walking with the prettiest girl in the village. Every youth wanted to be seen going out on the water with the prettiest girl in the village. And she wanted to keep all of them competing for her favors. Even Sun Cloud. So, whenever he pressed her to marry him, she put him off for a while by asking him to prove his love for her. Always she set him an almost impossible task. For it pleased her to have someone making a stupendous effort to win her. Also, an almost impossible task kept her very plain suitor away for a long time.

First, she wanted a white sea otter pelt. "It is my greatest desire," she told Sun Cloud. "I will never be happy without a white sea otter pelt. So, if you really love me, you will get one for me."

"A *white* sea otter pelt?" the youth said in dismay. For only once had anybody in the village seen a white sea otter pelt. And that was long ago, when Na-na-simgat's wife had been carried off to the Mountain of Qwawk. But Snow Flower wanted one. So Sun Cloud tried to get it for her.

For a year he went out again and again, searching and searching the sea. And perhaps the Great Sea Otter finally took pity on the young man. For at long last he did find a white sea otter. And he took its pelt back to Snow Flower.

"Here is your white sea otter pelt," he said with great joy. "Now you will marry me?"

"Well . . . not yet," Snow Flower protested, smiling sweetly at him. For she had no intention of marrying him and so cutting off the flattering attentions of her other suitors. Yet she wanted to keep him, too, making other girls jealous.

Sun Cloud was most unhappy. But Snow Flower was so beautiful that he still desired her. He pursued her until she thought of another way to put him off for a while.

"What I really crave . . ." she said, one day while they were watching the wild geese pass high overhead in their great Vs, "What I really crave is a goose feast in early summer when the roses are blooming."

"In early summer?" Sun Cloud said in dismay. For by early summer the geese would all be in their summer camps far to the north. No, not all, he remembered. There was a certain lake where geese sometimes came in early summer when the roses were blooming. And if that was the only way to prove his love for her, he would get the geese for the feast she craved.

At once he went out and shot a passing goose with his arrow. Carefully he skinned it, dried it, and stuffed it so that it seemed to be truly alive once more. And when the time came, he took this decoy to the certain lake. He set it out among the reeds. Then he called like a wild goose. And when other geese answered his call, he shot several of them. Again and again he put his decoy out among the reeds. Again and again he called like a wild goose. And when other geese answered his call, he shot several of them, too. Until, at last, he had enough geese for the feast Snow Flower wanted.

"Here are the geese for your summer feast," he said with great joy. "Now you will marry me?"

"Well . . . not yet," Snow Flower protested, smiling sweetly at him. For she still had no intention of marrying him and so cutting off the flattering attentions of her other suitors.

"You don't ever mean to marry me," Sun Cloud
burst out. "You are trifling with me."

"Oh no, no, no, no!" she protested, smiling at him
more sweetly than ever. "I just want to be sure that
you truly love me. Sun Cloud, do you love me well
enough to do *anything* for me?" she asked him.

"Anything!" he vowed.

"Anything?" she insisted. And she racked her
brains to think of a task that he could not accomplish.
For Sun Cloud was becoming a nuisance to her.

Her glance chanced to fall on a slave, on the close-
cropped head of a slave. That was the way a slave
was identified after his capture—by his cropped hair.

"You would do *anything* for me?" she asked again,
hiding the malicious light in her eyes.

"Try me!" he challenged.

"You would even . . . cut off your hair for me?"
she asked him.

"Cut off my hair?" Sun Cloud burst out in dismay.

But he had vowed *anything!* "You will see," he
told her. And he strode off.

"I will see," Snow Flower whispered to herself.
She knew that not even Sun Cloud would do such a
thing, even to win her. And she would be free of him
without it seeming to be her fault. .

But winning Snow Flower had become such an
obsession with Sun Cloud that he really would do
anything to prove his love for her. Now he went to
his best friend. "Cut off my hair!" he ordered his best
friend.

"Cut . . . off . . . your hair?" the friend said,

aghast at such an order. "You are not a slave, Sun Cloud."

"I am a slave to Snow Flower, as I will prove to her," Sun Cloud answered. "Cut off my hair!"

His best friend tried to reason with him. But Sun Cloud was beyond reason. "Cut off my hair!" he ordered.

So the friend did.

And now, with his hair cropped short around his very, very plain face, Sun Cloud went to Snow Flower.

"You *have* cut off your hair!" she said, aghast at what he had done. "You have made yourself a slave."

"Your slave," he agreed. "Now you will marry me?"

"Marry a SLAVE!" she cried out, aghast at the very thought. And she ran from him in horror.

As if scales had dropped from his eyes, Sun Cloud saw that she had never intended to marry him. She had merely used him to feed her vanity. Lost in despair at the cruel ending of a dream, he raced off into the dripping wet wilderness. Wanting only to hide his shame from the village, he went on and on and on and on.

ONLY MOUSE WOMAN knew where he went. For, as usual, she was watching the world with her big, busy, mouse eyes.

"Should I? . . . Or shouldn't I?" she asked herself, after she had watched the shamed young man for some time.

And being the busiest little busybody in the Place,

she didn't take long to answer herself. "I *should* do what I have in mind."

But what she had in mind was marrying Sun Cloud to the daughter of the Sun. "I don't really approve of marriages between humans and supernatural beings," she reminded herself sharply.

"But there are times when nothing else will do," she answered herself. And her nose twitched.

"Besides . . ." Besides, the daughter of the Sun had been teasing for centuries to be allowed to spend a few years among the humans to see how it was in the beautiful little village when storm clouds hid it from Sky view. So she would gladly come to the village long enough to remind young people that beauty without warmth and kindness was like an elegantly carved food box without food; it was like a handsome spirit-mask without the spirit. When that had been accomplished, she would be bright enough to think of a proper way to vanish. With no harm done.

"I should do what I have in mind," Mouse Woman told herself. Very firmly.

So IT WAS THAT, as Sun Cloud was following an animal trail one day, he saw a lame mouse trying to climb over a big log.

"Poor little mouse!" he said; for Sun Cloud could never be so lost in his own troubles that he could not see the troubles of others. He lifted the lame mouse gently over the log, and watched it with compassionate eyes as it disappeared into a thicket of tall ferns.

Then he heard a voice call out from behind the ferns. "Come in, my dear," it invited in an imperious little squeak.

Surprised by the command, Sun Cloud parted the ferns. And there, to his amazement, was a house decorated all over with Mouse totems.

"Come in, my dear!" the imperious squeak repeated.

So he went in. And there was the tiniest grandmother he had ever seen. She had a field mouse robe on her little shoulders.

"Mouse Woman!" he cried out, and now his eyes shone. For it was well known that Mouse Woman was always a friend to young people in distress. "Mouse Woman!" he said again, with proper respect. For Mouse Woman was also a narnauk.

"Sit down, my dear!" Mouse Woman invited. "You have been kind to me, so I will repay your kindness." *Though there is no wool in this for my ravelly little fingers*, she thought, watching the swing of his caribou skin earrings. *No matter. It must be done.*

Sun Cloud sank down onto a mat beside the fire. And he gratefully took the roasted salmon the tiny narnauk gave him.

"You shall marry a daughter of the Sun," Mouse Woman told him. Just like that. For, of course, by now it had all been arranged.

"Marry?" he burst out. Then his own interest in the idea surprised him. "A daughter of the Sun?" he went on, astounded at *such* a marriage.

Nothing less!" Mouse Woman warned him. "They

will try to offer you less. But you will know when it is the daughter of the Sun."

"She will say, 'Well . . . not yet!'?" Sun Cloud said with one last burst of bitterness. Then, aghast at the way the little narnauk's nose twitched, he added, "I will know her." She would be golden-bright, he knew, and warm as a flood of sunbeams. "But . . ." But would such a Sky princess want to marry so plain a human?

Mouse Woman answered his thoughts. "She wants to live among humans for a time. . . . Only for a time," she cautioned.

"Even for a time!" he answered. "How do I find her, Grandmother?" He leaped up, eager to begin his journey.

Mouse Woman gave him careful directions. "Follow this trail until you come to a high mountain. Then climb to the very top. But never look back! And there you will see another trail, climbing higher yet. That you must follow. And never look back!"

"I will never look back," he promised.

"But first, my dear, you must rest. It will be a long, hot climb. Only the valiant can win a daughter of the Sun," she warned him.

So Sun Cloud rested. And as he rested, he kept asking Mouse Woman about the daughter of the Sun.

"She is more beautiful than any girl you have ever seen," the tiny narnauk assured him. "Warm and bright as a sunbeam."

Thinking about her, Sun Cloud rapidly lost his old longing for Snow Flower who, he now realized, was as warm and bright as a snowbank on the mountain. "My hair is growing longer," he noted with pleasure.

He knew that he was a very, very, very plain suitor. But at least he would not look like a slave when he met the daughter of the Sun.

Next morning he started off.

"Never look back!" Mouse Woman called after him.

"I will never look back," he promised. And to prove it, he did not even look back as he answered the tiny narnauk.

Soon he reached the mountain and began to climb. And though startling calls and fearsome noises sounded behind him, he never looked back. He climbed on and on and on and on, while the Sun beat fiercely down on him. At last he reached the top of the mountain.

Still he did not look back. He looked ahead to where the Sun shone so fiercely that he tilted his woven hat down over his eyes to shade them. And suddenly there was a trail in front of him, leading onward and upward toward the Sun. A trail that seemed as bright and gossamer as a rainbow, and almost as narrow.

Sun Cloud caught his breath. He had a wild urge to whirl round and race back down the mountain. But he did not even glance back. Instead, he took a great breath of mountain air and stepped out along the airy trail. For only the valiant could win a daughter of the Sun.

And a very strange thing happened. As he walked along, something gave swiftness to his stride. Almost he walked on the wind; and the wind carried him toward a dazzling village.

Sun Cloud could not do more than glance at the

houses, in fear of their brightness. He tilted his hat lower yet to shade his eyes more. And he trembled in awe for some time before he could find his voice to call out.

In answer, a man came from one of the houses. "What is your wish?" he asked Sun Cloud.

"A . . . a daughter of the Sun," the young man blurted out. Only the thought of Mouse Woman's twitching nose gave him the courage to say that much.

"Come with me!"

Sun Cloud followed the man into one of the dazzling houses. Inside it was more restful to eyes accustomed to storm-darkened seas and rain-shrouded forests. The brightness of the Sun was shut out.

"What is your wish?" a chief asked him from the rear of the fire.

"I wish . . . to . . . marry . . . a daughter of the Sun," Sun Cloud answered, more and more aware of the great thing he was asking. For why should a radiant daughter of the Sun marry a youth who was not only merely human, but also the plainest of humans?

Mouse Woman could have told him. But Mouse Woman did not make her appearance.

The Chief nodded. He signalled to one of the women. And she went out into the dazzling light of the Sun's village.

By and by she returned with a beautiful young lady.

Sun Cloud caught his breath at sight of her. He blinked his eyes. For she was as sparkling as a frosted tree in winter sunlight. She was as sparkling as a berry bush after the rain, when every trembling drop was a glittering point of light. She was as sparkling as a night sky in clear weather.

But she was not the daughter of the Sun, he knew. For she had a certain coldness.

"A daughter of the Stars," the Chief said, as though hearing the youth's thoughts. And he signalled her departure, with the woman.

After a while the woman returned with another beautiful young lady.

Again Sun Cloud caught his breath at sight of her. Again he blinked his eyes. For she was as shiningly pale as a birch tree in moonlight. She was as lovely as the Moon's path across a mountain lake. But she was not the daughter of the Sun, he knew. For she had a certain coldess.

"A daughter of the Moon," the Chief said, as though hearing the youth's thoughts. And he signalled her departure, with the woman.

And now Sun Cloud's heart began to thump in his chest, like a drum. He almost held his breath as he watched the doorway, waiting for the coming of the daughter of the Sun.

And when she came, a lovely warmth and brightness seemed to flood the vast windowless house. When she looked at him, it was as though gentle sunbeams swept over him and through him.

"You are the daughter of the Sun," he said; and his voice was low with awe of her beauty. For as Mouse Woman had said, she was more beautiful than any girl he had ever seen.

"And you are Sun Cloud," she answered, "who

will marry me and take me home to your beautiful little village." She actually sounded eager.

"You . . . will? . . ." He could scarcely believe that so radiant a young lady would indeed marry a very, very, very plain suitor. But then, he did not know that for centuries she had been teasing to live among the humans on the rain coast to see how it was in the beautiful little village when storm clouds hid it from Sky view.

"I will marry you," she assured him.

And she did marry him. She did go to his village with him. Together they slid to earth down a long golden sunbeam. They walked along the dripping trail toward his home and it was as though the Sun himself brightened the forest and set the birds singing.

When they reached the village, people crowded about them in joy at Sun Cloud's return. Then they drew back in awe of the beautiful girl with him.

"This is my wife, Sunbeam," Sun Cloud said proudly.

"Your wife?" Snow Flower snapped. Her dark eyes narrowed. For now, she knew, she was no longer the prettiest girl in the village.

As the days went by, as the moons waxed and waned, the people took Sunbeam to their hearts. For her smile seemed to brighten the great windowless houses, heal the sick, dry the tears of grieving people, and remind the young that beauty without warmth and kindness was like an elegantly painted food box without food; it was like a handsome spirit-mask without the spirit. Everybody loved her.

Everybody, except Snow Flower.

Lost in jealousy of Sun Cloud's radiant wife, Snow Flower became more and more like the mosquitoes that people avoided. One by one her suitors left her to marry kinder girls. Until at last there was only one young man in the village who wanted her—because no other girl wanted him. So Snow Flower married him.

"I KNEW I SHOULD," Mouse Woman told herself one day as she watched from behind a blossoming salmonberry bush.

"I knew I should," she repeated. And she took a small hop, skip, and jump just to express her pleasure. For it was all very satisfying. The daughter of the Sun had at last found out how it was in the beautiful little village when storm clouds hid it from Sky view. A helpful one had been helped; while one who had tried to make others jealous had herself been made jealous. Making things equal. And the young had been reminded that beauty without warmth and kindness was like an elegantly painted food box without food; it was like a handsome spirit-mask without the spirit.

"I knew I should," Mouse Woman told herself once more.

Indeed, there were times when doing the improper thing was the only way to bring proper order back to a village disturbed by a mischief-maker.

But she did wish there had been some wool in it for her ravelly little fingers.

7

Mouse Woman and the Tooth

THERE WAS a rumor about Mouse Woman.

It wasn't one of the stories they told about her in the feasthouses. It was just a rumor that the old people whispered to one another when they were chuckling together about things *they* had done in their own childhood; when they were remembering the stories *they* had made up to get themselves out of trouble. And they didn't actually believe the rumor.

After all, who could think that Mouse Woman had ever been anything but the spirited, imperious little busybody they all called Grandmother? Who could ever think she had once been a girl-narnauk playing with other children? And who could ever ever think SHE had once made up a story to get herself out of trouble? Or had even gotten into trouble in the first place?

"Of course, it's only a rumor," they reminded one another. And anyway, it had happened—if indeed it had happened!—in the time of very, very, very Long Before. Long Before some of the Real People had migrated southward along the Coast to build their handsome totem pole villages. Long Before Mouse Woman herself had moved southward into the Place-of-Supernatural-Beings to watch the world with her big, busy, mouse eyes.

According to the rumor, the small-girl-narnauk named Mouse Woman was living with her Mouse People relatives far to the north of the Place. And one day she was out playing with the other children. According to the rumor, she was running and squeaking and catching a streaming kelp bulb when one of her playmates noticed something.

"Mouse Woman!" the friend squeaked. "You've lost a tooth."

"Yes," Mouse Woman agreed. And she clamped her mouth shut to end the conversation.

"But . . . it wasn't even loose yesterday," her friend insisted. "It wasn't wiggly or anything."

"Wasn't it?" Mouse Woman asked, as if she couldn't quite remember.

"So! What happened to your tooth?" the friend insisted.

"Well . . ." Mouse Woman looked up at the sky while she tried to think of a good way a small girl could lose a tooth that hadn't even been loose or wiggly the day before. And, looking at the sky, she suddenly thought of Envious-One, the mischievous little being who was always doing something spiteful to children. Or at least he was always being blamed for doing something that a more proper little being would never have done.

"Envious-One did it," Mouse Woman announced.

"Oh!" her friend squeaked. "What did he do?"

"Well . . . " Mouse Woman went on, quickly thinking what Envious-One could have done. "He shot at me from the Sky and knocked out my tooth with one of those little arrows."

"Oh!" The friend looked properly indignant about Envious-One's dreadful deed.

"And it hurts terribly," Mouse Woman went on. For she was beginning to enjoy her own story. "In fact," she went on, "I think I'm going to die." She put both hands over her mouth to prove that it hurt so terribly that she might even die the way the Real People died.

"Oh!" her friend squeaked, looking even more indignant about Envious-One's dreadful deed. "Well . . . you mustn't die outside." So, putting an arm around her hurt friend, she led Mouse Woman into the house.

"My dear! What has happened?" Mouse Woman's mother cried out.

"Envious-One did it," the friend said. "He shot at her from the Sky and knocked out her tooth with one of those little arrows."

Mouse Woman showed her teeth to prove that he had indeed done the dreadful deed.

"Lie down, my dear!" her mother said. And she covered Mouse Woman with a rabbit skin robe. "We'll send for Grandmother."

"Oh, no!" Mouse Woman squeaked. "I mean . . . please don't trouble Grandmother!" Grandmother

was a wise old woman with very, very sharp eyes.

But her mother sent for Grandmother.

"My dear! What has happened?" Grandmother asked when she saw Mouse Woman lying under the rabbit skin robe.

"Envious-One did it," Mouse Woman's mother answered. "He shot at her from the Sky and knocked out her tooth with one of those little arrows."

Reluctantly Mouse Woman showed her teeth to prove that he had indeed done the dreadful deed. But she quickly shut her mouth and her eyes, too, with the pain of it all. For Grandmother had very, very sharp eyes.

"We must do something about this," Grandmother announced. "Fetch me a drum, Ermine Woman!"

Ermine Woman fetched her the drum, and Grandmother began to beat on it very, very softly, for spirit guidance.

Then she stopped drumming. "First, we must find the tooth," she announced. And she sent Ermine Woman to tell all the small children in the village to search for the lost tooth.

They searched and searched and searched and searched. But no one could find the lost tooth. And they all went back to the house with Ermine Woman to report to Grandmother.

"Fetch me the drum again, Ermine Woman!" Grandmother ordered.

Ermine Woman fetched her the drum, and once again Grandmother began to beat on it very, very softly, for spirit guidance.

Then she stopped drumming. "Perhaps I can find the tooth," she said, "for I have very, very sharp eyes. Come with me, Ermine Woman, while the children wait here with Mouse Woman."

And off they went; while the children waited in the house with Mouse Woman, who seemed to be looking more and more distressed, as if indeed she *might* die the way the Real People died.

"Ermine Woman," Grandmother said. "I think our small girl has been pilfering the stone pine-nut cakes." For it was well known that Mouse Woman was very, very fond of stone pine-nut cakes. Grandmother led the way to a small house where many food boxes were stored.

"Search in that box!" Grandmother ordered, pointing to a large box of stone pine-nut cakes.

So Ermine Woman searched. And by and by she held up a small hard cake that had been well nibbled around the edges.

Grandmother took the nibbled cake. "Now find the tooth!" she ordered.

And Ermine Woman found the tooth. It was right near the spot where the hard little cake had been nibbled.

"I think our small girl has been pilfering the stone pine-nut cakes," Grandmother said. And though her eyes twinkled a little, her voice was very stern. For GREED was the Great Sin—especially for a young person as high-ranking as Mouse Woman.

They went back to the house with Grandmother hiding the nibbled cake under her fur robe, and Ermine Woman holding up the lost tooth.

"You've found her tooth!" several children squeaked. And they crowded about to see it.

Mouse Woman shut her eyes *not* to see it. And now she was looking even more distressed, as if she might indeed die the way the Real People died.

"You've found her tooth!"

"We've found *a* tooth," Grandmother agreed. "But it may not be Mouse Woman's." After all, there were many small children in the room with teeth missing. So she ordered Ermine Woman to try it first in the tooth-gaps of the other children.

And Ermine Woman went from child to child, from tooth-gap to tooth-gap, trying to fit the tooth into the empty socket. But the gap was always too large or too small.

"Then it must be Mouse Woman's," Grandmother said. "Open your mouth, my dear!"

Reluctantly Mouse Woman opened her mouth. But she shut her eyes with the pain of it all. For Grandmother had very, very sharp eyes.

Ermine Woman placed the tooth in the tooth-gap. And it fitted perfectly into the empty socket.

"It's Mouse Woman's!" the children squeaked. "Where did you find it, Grandmother?"

"Where I found it, my dears," Grandmother answered. "Have no more concern for Mouse Woman. She will soon be well again. Go back to your game, children!"

So the children went out of the house to start running and squeaking and catching a streaming kelp bulb again.

"And now, my dear," Grandmother said, looking

down at the small-girl-narnauk lying under the rabbit skin robe. She showed the well nibbled stone pine-nut cake.

"Yes, Grandmother," Mouse Woman squeaked in a very, very small voice. She looked up at the wise old lady with big, unhappy eyes.

"Guess where I found the tooth, my dear!" Grandmother ordered.

"With . . . the . . . cake?" Mouse Woman guessed, as if it might indeed be just a guess.

"With the cake, my dear," Grandmother agreed. And she went off.

"Well!" her mother said sternly when Grandmother had gone. "You have been pilfering the stone pine-nut cakes. You!" Her "You!" was a most indignant squeak. For it was well known that GREED was the Great Sin. It was equally well known that a high-ranking girl must be an example to other people. And what girl among the Mouse People was as high-ranking as the girl who wore the great title of Mouse Woman?

"I might as well die," Mouse Woman squeaked, for it would be a dreadful thing if the other children ever found out that Mouse Woman was greedy. "What am I going to do?"

"Perhaps you should strangle yourself on a forked willow twig, my dear," her mother suggested, though of course she didn't mean it. It was just something Mouse People sometimes said to their children since it was well known that distressed Real Mice occasionally strangled themselves on a forked willow twig. It was equally well known that supernatural

Mouse People could never die.

"That's what I'll do," Mouse Woman announced, suddenly leaping up. Thankful for a way to escape, she rushed out of the house. And she stayed away for a very, very long time. So they'd all be sorry. But at last she crept back into the house.

"I couldn't find a forked willow twig," she told her mother.

"Then perhaps we had better just forget all about it, my dear," her mother suggested.

And, according to the rumor, Mouse Woman was very glad to forget all about it.

PERHAPS WE had better just forget all about it, too," the old people whispered to one another.

But they never did. They just kept on whispering the rumor to one another when they were chuckling together about things *they* had done in their own childhood; when they were remembering the stories *they* had made up to get themselves out of trouble. Still, they never did actually believe the rumor.

And anyway it had happened—if indeed it had happened!—in the time of very, very, very Long Before. Long Before Mouse Woman had begun watching the world with her big, busy, mouse eyes. Long Before she had begun helping people who had been tricked into trouble. Long Long Before she had developed the habit of tearing woolen tassels into a lovely, loose, nesty pile of wood with her ravelly little fingers.

STORY SOURCES

DURING THE PAST TWO CENTURIES, the rich native cultures of our Northwest Coast have almost vanished into the more dominant immigrant cultures. But, fortunately for us, there have always been concerned people to record the songs and the stories before they were forgotten.

Mouse Woman has been waiting for us to find her in the following collections:

1898. *The Mythology of the Bella Coola Indians*, collected by Franz Boas for The Jesup North Pacific Expedition publications, Memoirs of the American Museum of Natural History.

1899. *Tales from the Totems of the Hidery*, collected by James Deans for the Archives of the International Folk-lore Association.

1905. *Haida Texts*, collected by John Reed Swanton for The Jesup North Pacific Expedition publications, Memoirs of the American Museum of Natural History.

1908. *The Koryak*, collected by Waldemar Jochelson for The Jesup North Pacific Expedition publications, Memoirs of the American Museum of Natural History.

1909–1910. *Tsimshian Myths*, collected by Franz Boas for the Thirty-First Annual Report of the Bureau of American Ethnology to the Secretary of the Smithsonian Institution.

1953. *Haida Myths Illustrated in Argillite Carvings*, by Marius Barbeau, Bulletin No. 127, Anthropological Series No. 32, National Museum of Canada.

ABOUT THE AUTHOR

CHRISTIE HARRIS started her writing career when she was a young teacher and pursued it avidly while she reared five children in a British Columbia border town. Both her western surroundings and her family became grist for her writing mill.

Northwest Coast Indians and Western Canadian history provided material for *Once Upon a Totem, Once More Upon a Totem, West With the White Chiefs, Skyman on the Totem Pole?, Secret in the Stlalakum Wild* and *Raven's Cry,* a story of the Haida Indians that received the Book of the Year medal from the Canadian Association of Children's Librarians.

Her own children lent their stories of growing up to *Confessions of a Toe-Hanger* and *Let X Be Excitement. Figleafing Through History* was written with her daughter, Moira Johnston.

In *Mouse Woman and the Vanished Princesses* and these new Mouse Woman stories, Mrs. Harris has returned again to a first love, Northwest Indian lore.